BEAUTIFUL DARKNESS

VICTORIA ZAK

VICTORIA ZAK ROMANCE

Copyright

Beautiful Darkness - Victoria Zak
Copyright 2018 by Victoria Zak

All rights reserved. Except as permitted under the U.S. Copyright Act 1976, no part of this publication may be reproduced, distributed, or transmitted in any form or by any means, or stored in a database or retrieval system without prior written permission of the author and publisher.

All characters, events, and locations in this book are fictitious. Any similarity to real persons, dead or living, is coincidental and not intended by the author.

Cover Design: JAB Designs

Editing: Violetta Rand

Created with Vellum

CONTENTS

Sign up for Victoria Zak's newsletter at her website to
receive a free ebook copy of her
Guardians of Scotland novella
Highland Destiny

You'll also find additional special offers, bonus content and
info on new releases.

www.victoriazakromance.com
victoria@victoriazakromance.com

PROLOGUE

14TH-CENTURY SCOTLAND
  Dornoch Castle

Wee Masie Keith rubbed the sleep from her eyes and yawned as she sat up in bed looking around the moon-lit bedchamber she shared with her two sisters. As she squinted through the shadows, she saw her older sister, Leana, sitting on the window ledge, staring off into the moor. *What is she looking at?* They were supposed to be asleep.

Quietly, so not to wake her oldest sister, Masie padded across the cold stone floor to the window and tapped Leana's shoulder. Her sister jumped.

"Masie." She held her hand to her chest. "Ye scared the devil out of me."

"What are ye doing?" Masie asked.

Leana waved her off. "Go back to bed before you wake Adaira."

As the youngest, only seven summers old, her sisters

were always telling her what to do, especially Adaira. She could hear her nagging voice in her mind, "Masie, ye shouldn't run down the corridor." "Masie, eat yer vegetables." She knew they were only looking out for her best interest, but her spirit was free, sometimes getting her into trouble, especially with her da, the Doughall.

Masie batted her eyelashes, swaying back-and-forth. "Pleeease, let me seeee."

Leana smiled and pulled her onto her lap. "Such a curious, wee one ye are." She gathered Masie's sleep-tangled hair in her hands. "I'm looking for a shooting star."

"Why?"

Leana kissed the top of her head. "My sweet, innocent Masie."

Masie knew wishing upon a star meant you wanted to change your fate or wish for something you don't have. But what she didn't know was why. Something was bothering her sister, she could feel it. "Please tell me."

Leana exhaled as she searched the night sky. "The Doughall hurts Mum, and I'm afraid his attention is set on Adaira now. I need a shooting star to wish him away."

Every time she encountered Doughall, she'd hide behind her sisters, making herself as small as possible so she wouldn't be noticed. She'd shake with fear at the thunder in his voice when he yelled. Her heart broke more and more with every bruise she saw on her mum's face. No husband or father should treat his family with such hate. She despised the man.

Masie faced Leana and a tear rolled off her cheek. She wrapped her arms around her sister. "We can't let the bastard hurt us anymore."

"Masie!" Leana gasped at her language. "That's no way for a wee lass to talk."

"Mayhap, we could wish a big bear would eat him." Masie sniffled.

"Or for an arrow to pierce his heartless chest." Adaira stood next to them with her arms crossed as she, too, gazed into the sky.

"I'm sorry, did we wake ye?" Leana asked.

"Nay, I can no' sleep."

Masie looked up at Adaira, a bruise marred her left cheek. Aye, she might have been innocent, but she knew more than her sisters thought she did. She'd heard her mother's cries as her da beat her. She'd seen the cuts and bruises left behind in his drunken rages as he condemned her as an unfit wife for not giving him a son. Sorrow filled her mum's eyes and the situation was worsening y. Aye, the Doughall was a bad man.

The three sisters sat together, Masie in the middle, gazing at the twinkling stars. Wee Masie squeezed her eyes closed, praying hard to the gods a shooting star would magically appear. *Please, if ye grant me this one wish, I promise to eat all my cabbage.* She wrinkled her nose but her promise was good.

After a while, the girls grew impatient.

"'Tis an auld wives' tale. We should go to sleep," Adaira said as she skulked to her bed.

Disappointed, Masie bowed her head and kicked at the stone wall. "Stupid stars."

All of a sudden, Leana jumped to her feet. "Did you see that?"

"Leana, enough wit' yer daft tales. Ye should no' put these silly ides in Masie's head. Ye can no' change yer fate."

"Nay, look." Leana pointed down into the moor.

Curiosity-stricken, Masie looked. She couldn't believe her eyes. "Will-o-the wisp," she gasped.

Adaira stomped over to the window. "This is quite enough."

"Look," Masie exclaimed, jumping up and down.

Adair froze, then whispered, "Fairy fire."

Leana ran toward the door, only stopping to put on her shoes.

"Where are ye going?" Adaira asked.

"I'm going to change our fate." Leana smiled at Adaira.

"What? Leana, have ye gone mad? Remember Mum said to never trust fairy fire. Besides, ye do no' want to wake Doughall. If he catches ye out of bed, he'll lash ye."

Ignoring her sister, Leana swung the door open and ran down the corridor.

Masie glanced at Adaira and grinned. "Dinnae ye want to help Mum? Doughall must die." Masie bolted from the bedchamber, following Leana. "Wait for me."

As fast as her legs could go, Leana dashed down the stairs. For a fortnight, long into the wee hours of the morn, she'd sat and waited for brightest star to appear. Tonight, it was no coincidence her wish had come true. Their fate was going to change.

She couldn't bear to see her mother suffer any longer. Witnessing Adaira suffering the same way was inexcusable. At all costs, she'd protect her family. She pushed open the castle doors and slipped out with Masie close behind. She rounded the corner to the east side of the tower and came to a halt.

A cloud of white glowing starbursts flickered and hovered above the ground, dancing in the air. Soft chattering came from the light and sounded like people whispering. Leana listened closely, but she couldn't understand what they were saying. A calm feeling surged through her body.

Out of breath, Masie caught up to her. "Adaira thinks we've gone mad."

"I dinnae care. My wish was answered."

The two girls were mesmerized by the will-o-the-wisp.

"I have a bad feeling about this," Adaira said.

"Och, Sister." Leana winked at Adaira. "I'm glad ye caught up with us. Have faith."

The fairy fire floated toward the forest, illuminating the pathway, inviting them in like a welcoming hand. Leana picked up the pace, following the eerie light. She knew all her troubles would soon be resolved. Every fiber of her being pulsed with certainty that the fae would grant her wish.

As the sisters ran deeper into the woods, tree branches twisted together, creating a thick canopy. Leana slowed down suddenly, uncertain of the danger ahead. The shimmering lights hovered inside a tunnel formed by the trees.

"Don't be afraid," the voices murmured.

Leana gasped. She understood. Tamping down her fear, she ran ahead, stepping inside the tunnel. Suddenly, the wind blew leaves and dirt about, causing Leana to lose sight of the fairy fire. Her sisters coughed from behind her.

Adaira wrapped Masie in her arms. "I told ye this was a bad idea."

"Shh. Do you hear it?"

"Nay. Masie is frightened. We must leave before it's too late," Adaira warned.

"'Tis water." Leana pushed deeper into the tunnel, leaping over fallen logs and dodging low-lying branches.

As they reached the end of the tunnel, the forest opened up, revealing a crystal-waterfall. It emptied into a pool surrounded by black rocks. The girls stood for a long moment, dazzled by the splendor. It was as if they had stepped into a different realm.

Leana gave Adaira a sideways grin. "I told ye to have faith."

Adaira rolled her eyes.

They walked to the water's edge and kneeled.

"Remember the fairy story Mum told us?" Leana asked.

"Aye," Masie said. "In order to see the fae, one must wash their eyes and drink from the fairy pool."

"Verra good, Masie." Leana smiled.

"Are ye sure about this?" Adaira asked.

Leana cupped her hands into the bubbling blue. "Aye."

"The water is cold," Masie complained.

"And refreshing." Leana winked at Masie as she sampled the water.

After they finished drinking, they splashed water on their faces. Leana glanced over at Adaira. Although her sister didn't believe in such nonsense, Leana could see the hope in her eyes. Would their family finally be free of Doughall?

Anxious, Leana stood and quickly dried her face on her nightgown. Where was the pixie who was going to grant her wish?

"Where's this fae, Leana?" Adaira asked sarcastically.

"She has to be here." Leana searched a clump of tall grass next to the fairy pool. "Fairies are mischievous. She must be hiding."

They left no stone unturned.

Masie looked behind trees calling out to the fae. "Fairy. Oh, fairy."

Unfortunately, there were no fae folk to be found.

"I'm through with yer games, Leana Keith. We're leaving, now," Adaira demanded.

Leana blew a lock of red hair from her face. *Where could she be?* She'd wished upon a star. The tale had to be true. Disappointment and dread crept up her spine. She couldn't return home without her wish. Their fates must change.

A gust of cold wind blew straight through Leana's nightgown, chilling her to the bone. The girls huddled together, shivering as dark clouds overshadowed the moon. Popping sounds echoed behind them. Leana looked over her shoulder. The waterfall had crystalized, blue ice covered the fairy pool.

"What's happening?" Adaira asked.

"I dinnae know," Leana answered.

Snow collected on the treetops and blanketed the ground. Frightened, the girls clung together as they watched the world around them transform into a winter wonderland.

The forest was shrouded in a heavy mist, making it hard for the girls to see. Wind blew violently, chilling their skin and whipping their hair. It wasn't supposed to be winter yet.

In the distance, the mist parted and a woman slowly rose from the ground. She had creamy white skin and her hair was black as night. Her sheer gown was covered with leaves and ivy. Twigs shimmered and twisted into a high collar which looked as if they had sprouted from her shoulders. With magical grace, as if the woman floated, she made her way forward.

"The winter fae queen," Leana whispered.

"She's pretty," Masie said in awe.

The sisters gasped as three huge stags with riders joined the queen.

Leana couldn't stop staring at the riders. She'd never

seen men of this stature before. Strong jawlines without a whisker on their faces and plump lips. They had long, black hair and dark markings that swirled up their arms and chests. One man mesmerized her with his amber eyes and flawless skin. Although Leana was young, the man stirred uncomfortable feelings inside her.

"What brings such tender creatures to my woods?" the queen asked.

Leana couldn't speak. Her wish had indeed come true.

"We come to change our fate," Adaira spoke up.

The queen studied Adaira. "Change your fate?"

"Aye," Masie chimed in. "We wished upon a star." She stepped closer to the queen. "We want to help our mum."

The queen cocked her head as she looked down at the child. "Aren't you a pretty thing." She touched Masie's cheek with a long, bony finger.

Adaira pulled her little sister back into her arms, but when she did, the queen's fingernail scratched Masie's face. Masie held her cheek and hid behind Adaira.

The fairy tasted Masie's blood, licking her fingertip. Her eyes widened as she looked at the girls.

"Your majesty." Leana curtsied. "Can I speak freely?"

The queen nodded.

"What my sisters are trying to say is, we need yer help. Our father is a verra mean man and he hurts our mum terribly. We've come to you to change our fate, to save our mum."

The queen studied her for a moment before she answered. "Do you clearly understand what you ask of me?"

"Aye."

"In order to grant your wish, I must get something in return."

"Anything," Leana proclaimed innocently.

"Leana." Adaira elbowed her sister. "Ye can no' promise that."

"What is it you ask of me?" the queen queried.

Masie peaked out from behind Adaira. "Doughall must die."

The queen bent down and motioned for Masie to step forward. She took her hands in hers. "Such strong words for a little girl."

"Please, we need your help," Leana begged.

The queen straightened. "It's the rule of the Unseelie in order to take a life, we must gain a life. One of you will have to come with me and live in my kingdom and learn our ways."

"I will do whatever ye ask," Leana pleaded.

"Nay." Adaira faced her sister. "There has to be another way."

"Sister, I can no' bear to see any more pain. I must do this."

Adaira glanced at the queen, considering her suspiciously, then stared deep into Leana's eyes. "Do ye understand the Unseelie? They are wicked. Remember Mum said to stay away, to keep on the path of good."

"Good? There's none back home. Doughall will only get worse. Please, Adaira, I have to do this."

Reluctantly, Adaira nodded. "I should be the one to go."

"Nay." Masie hugged Adaira tightly. "Ye can no' leave me."

"There's only one solution." Leana looked down at Masie. She'd do anything to keep her safe. "Whatever our fate is, we stand together."

After the words left her mouth, she waited for Adaira's response. Either way, she was seeing her wish through. She understood Adaira's apprehension. If she decided to take

Masie back home, she could rest easy knowing Doughall would never harm them again.

"Together," Adaira agreed.

"Ye dinnae have to do this, Adaira."

"Aye, I do."

Leana stepped forward and addressed the queen. "We'll all three come with ye, but ye must promise to kill Laird Keith so no harm befalls our mum ever again."

The queen's eyes grew dark. "I've always wanted children, for I cannot bear my own. I'll grant your wish. Girls, come." She motioned for Adaira and Masie to join her. "Hold out your hands."

The girls obeyed.

The Queen pricked their fingers with her sharp fingernail, then she pricked hers. Blood trailed down her hand as she held it up. She nodded to girls. "Place our fingers together."

They pressed their fingers against the queens.

"We're bound by blood," the queen said. "This oath can't be broken."

A tree rustled and a woman ran out of the forest. "Girls, what have ye done?"

"Mum!" Masie ran toward her mother.

The queen raised her fisted hand in the air. Masie fell to the ground in agonizing pain.

Before Masie's mum could reach her, Masie was captured by one of the queen's guards. "They're mine now. You've kept the truth from them long enough. It's time they become what they are destined to be."

"Nay. Ye tricked them. They are sweet and innocent. Ye must have mercy. They are goodhearted. Nothing like you."

The queen grabbed her by the chin. "They are blood

drinkers, *Baobhan sith*. You can't deny their fate." The queen turned and walked away, gathering Masie in her arms.

Leana and Adaira followed the queen, for they had no choice. They were each placed behind one of the riders on the stags. As they headed deep into the forest, Leana looked back at her mother, who was on her knees, crying out.

A tear trickled down Leana's cheek. "Mum, I love ye."

1

Ten years later
Samhain: The festival of the dead
Dornoch Castle

Masie knelt in front of the candle-lit shrine inside the stone alter, holding her mother's brooch in her hands. She missed her mum terribly and her heart ached to see her once again. A tear fell from her cheek as she remembered the day she had left home with her sisters. Her mother had died because of their mistakes.

It was the third night celebrating the dead and she still hadn't seen her mother's spirit. Every night, she prayed and lit candles, but it did nothing to help. Mayhap, her mother was still mad at her for leaving. This was Masie's punishment.

Gripping the brooch tight, she closed her eyes, imaging a time when she was happy. A perfect picture of her mother and sisters holding hands and dancing in a circle together vividly came alive. The smell of pine from the forest washed through her. Sunlight filtered through the clouds and warmed her skin as they laughed and sang. Masie breathed in. She could still smell the scent of heather that lingered about her mother.

By the gods, she missed her.

"Mum, I'm so sorry. Please forgive the heartache I've brought ye. We only wanted ye safe." Masie lowered her head, resting it on her steepled hands and kissed the brooch as she prayed.

"Go forth upon yer journey from this world. May the sun always shine down upon ye. May yer soul find happiness and grief no more. O' Mother, O' Maiden, O' Crone of Wisdom, I pray ye watch over my mum and lead her into the afterworld."

The candle flickered. Masie lifted her head, watching the flame's shadow dance up the stone wall. Could this be a sign? Had her mother finally heard her prayer?

"Mum," Masie whispered.

A cold wind blew out the candles. Disappointed, Masie hung her head.

The darkness didn't scare her. In fact, it soothed her. The ten harrowing years she'd spent with the fae queen had made her come to find peace in darkness. It was a shock at first to discover she was something other than human. As soon as the queen lifted the shielding spell Masie's mother had placed on her, the pain was relentless. Too weak, she spent day-after-day in bed struck with fever and stomach cramps. Her sisters, just as sick, took care of her. There were times when Masie wanted to take her own life. The pain was that unbearable.

Masie shook free from those ghastly memories. Last Samhain, the girls escaped the fae queen and returned home only to hear her mother had died right after the laird's mysterious death. The queen had failed in her promise, and Masie believed they had been tricked. Her mother was supposed to be safe. They had sold their souls to the queen and become monsters of the night—all for naught.

They'd accepted their newfound destiny, even took an oath to never talk about their curse or the time they had spent with the dark fae. They were blood drinkers now, eternally living in the shadows. Feared because their kind were unexplainable. Blessed with gifts viewed as evil, their blood healed the sick and prevented death. Masie swore she'd never give into the wickedness of the queen and would only drink from the dying.

Masie stood and tucked the brooch deep into the valley of her breasts. She opened the door and stepped out into the lively night where Clan Keith danced and feasted in celebration of the end of summer. As it grew late, folks headed back to their homes before the wicked came out to play.

It was rumored during Samhain that the fairy mounds opened and the veil between the dead and living was at its thinnest. although true, it amused her overhearing mothers warn their children of the dangerous creatures lurking outside. *If they had only seen the terrors I've seen.* Masie smiled inwardly. She couldn't hold back any longer. This was the time she felt most alive, when a different rhythm pulsed through the earth. Some kind of magic swam in the air, feeding her wild side.

Masie strolled through the moor. The flames from the bonfire raged up into the night sky and heated her skin. She stretched her arms up and twirled around, dancing to the hum of music inside her. Hiking up her dress, she joined the dancers around the fire. She felt free, even if it was only for one night. The threat of the queen finding them always loomed, but tonight, she welcomed the magic and threw caution to the wind.

Song after song played. Masie danced until she couldn't catch her breath. She excused herself and walked over to a table to get some wine. A strange sensation pricked her skin. Someone was watching her. Slowly, she whirled around. No one was there. She sighed with relief, often guilty of letting her imagination run amuck.

She returned to the bonfire to find a place to sit and wait for Leana, which meant she'd be here awhile, alone. Masie found a spot and sat down. Bringing the tankard of wine to her lips, the sensation returned. She froze. The hairs on the back of her neck bristled as a winged man standing on the other side of the fire stared at her. He ruffled his black wings and grinned wickedly. Masie gasped and dropped her cup. *The queen's guard! Shite!*

Tamping down the urge to panic, Masie averted her gaze. Mayhap she was seeing things. She dared to look back into the flames and when she did, the fae was gone. Yet, she couldn't shake the feeling something was wrong. Finding her sister was the only thing she could focus on.

Where could she be? She knew she hadn't retired for the night and had to be out here. But where?

Masie headed toward the blacksmith shop. It was the last place she hadn't looked. Given the way Leana had pranced off with two men earlier, and knowing her wild streak, she could most definitely be inside the building. Irritated by her sister's behavior, Masie banged on the door. "Leana! Are ye in there?"

No answer.

She knocked again. "Leana, I'm coming in."

As Masie entered, she prayed to the goddess she's find her sister. Not wanting to see her sister tangled with her lovers, Masie kept her gaze focused on the ground. "Leana, this is no' funny."

As she walked deeper inside, she saw a pair of trews and tunic scattered on the floor, then another pair of trews. *What the devil?*

Her search abruptly came to an end when Masie found her sister lying on the ground. "Leana!" Masie called out. "Why dinnae ye answer me?"

Masie gasped and held her hand over her mouth to stifle a scream. Leana was unconscious and lying between two naked men. Blood trailed down the corners of her sister's mouth.

"Leana." Masie knelt and checked her sister's neck for a pulse. Thank the gods, she was alive. "Wake up." She shook her.

Leana gradually came to. She held her head. "What happened?"

As Masie fetched Leana's dress, she tripped on one of the bodies. Her eyes grew wide when she saw two puncture wounds on the man's neck. Quickly, Masie checked him for any signs of life. He was cold. "Nay, Beathen," she whispered. *Shite!* "Leana, what have ye done?"

"What do ye mean?" Leana finished slipping her dress over her head. She looked down, then back at Masie. "I dinnae understand. I—"

"Sister, these men are dead.".

Terror stricken, Leana shivered in disbelief.

"That's the laird's son," Masie said in alarm.

"By the saints," Leana whispered. "Masie, I-I..."

Masie pulled her into a hug. "Shh."

"I didnae kill those men, Masie. Ye must believe me."

"I do, Sister." She smoothed her hand down Leana's red,

tangled hair. "We have to get out of here and tell Adaira. She'll know what to do."

"Aye."

Thankfully, the castle inhabitants were asleep as Masie and Leana snuck up the stairs to their bedchamber. Masie opened the door.

Adaira leapt off the bed. "Where have ye been? 'Tis late."

Dismayed, Leana shuffled to her bed and lay down.

"What's troubles her?" Adaira asked.

"Something verra bad has happened tonight," Masie's voice cracked.

"Tell me."

"I found Leana naked with two men."

"Aye," Adaira said as if the news was common enough.

"They had puncture wounds on the side of their necks."

"Aye." This time she sounded intrigued.

"They were dead."

"Dead?" Adaira exclaimed.

"One of the lads was the laird's son."

Adaira glared at Leana. "What have ye done?"

"She says she didnae kill them."

"And ye believe her? I warned ye two about the wickedness this night would bring." Adaira began to pace.

Masie couldn't believe what she'd seen. In her heart, she wanted to believe Leana was innocent, but she couldn't shake free from the memory of two dead bodies and the blood on Leana's lips.

"If Leana says she's innocent, then I trust she's telling the truth." Masie sat down next to Leana, watching Adaira pace in front of the window.

"The laird has sent his guards in search already," Adaira said, pointing out the window.

Masie joined her by the window. Seven Highlanders

perched high on their warhorses charged out of the front gates.

"We'll be hung for this," Adaira said dryly.

Masie knew it true. Ever since their return to Dornoch Castle, they had been under suspicion. Masie heard the whispers floating around the village square, accusing them of witchcraft. It all started one day at the market, a good deed gone bad.

A young child was dying of fever. Masie's heart had shattered when the child's mother begged her to help. Although Masie knew better than to meddle with death, she couldn't let the child die. So, she healed him. The word spread and they were under a watchful eye ever since.

"What are we going to do?" Masie asked.

"There's only one thing we can do. Leave," Adaira said.

Masie's heart sank into her stomach. Not because she had fond memories here, but the thought of traveling through the Highlands without proper shelter to hide away from the sun was a sure death to their kind. Fortunately, winter was coming, which meant the daylight hours grew ever shorter.

"Aye, we must go," Masie agreed.

Adaira pulled herself away from the widow and strode to her trunk. "Pack light. I'll ready the horses."

With haste, Masie packed a satchel for Leana who had fallen into a state of shock.

Masie took a green cloak from her trunk and draped it over her shoulders, then did the same for Leana. She kneeled in front of her sister. "We're in this together." She gave her a hug and was disappointed when Leana didn't respond.

Unaccustomed to Leana's weakened condition, it broke

her heart to see her usually carefree sister reduced to this. "Adaira is waiting for us with horses. Can ye ride?"

Leana met Masie's gaze and nodded.

"Good." Masie smiled. "Let's make haste." She helped her sister to her feet.

They made their way through the corridor and down the stairs to the great hall. A group of men marched upstairs. Quickly, Masie hid herself and Leana in the shadows. The laird had already sent for them. *This is no' good.* When it was clear, they pushed forward and ran out the castle door. They scurried across the bailey to the stables. As Masie entered, she found the stable marshal in a heap on the ground.

She looked up at Adaira, who was saddling the last horse. "Did ye have to kill him?"

"I didnae kill him. He's sleeping." She winked.

Maisie's heart pounded, fearful of being caught by guards. "The laird has already sent his men after us. I saw them searching upstairs as we left."

"We must go. Is she ready to ride?" Adaira nodded toward Leana.

"Aye." By the saints, she hoped so.

They mounted their horses and urged them into a thunderous gallop toward the shoreline and never looked back.

2

THE SISTERS HAD BEEN RIDING for days through the rocky moor, following the shoreline, and avoiding the sun. They hid in caves until nightfall or traveled in the rain. Today, the sky was gray, a perfect time to hunt. Adaira had promised when they came across the next village, they'd stay for a couple of nights. Sustaining their strength on small forest animals wasn't enough, they needed human blood.

With Adaira leading, they stopped next to a loch to let their horses drink and to relieve themselves. Masie dismounted and walked toward the water. She kneeled, dipping her cupped hands into the cold water. As she brought them to her lips, she smelled a familiar essence.

"There's blood in the water," she murmured. *Where's the body?*

Masie searched the shoreline. The odor wasn't only coming from the water, it filled the air. She followed the scent around the bend. *Where there's blood, there must be a body.*

Squinting, she tried to make out a heap of something floating in the surf. The iron smell brought her to a body.

Crows circled overhead as she examined the face-down body in the shallows. This couldn't be good. With caution, Masie dragged the corpse ashore, then rolled him over. She sat back on her heels and closely studied him.

His armor identified him as a warrior. And judging by the way he'd bled out, he'd met the pointy end of a sword. She wiped the blood from his chest plate. Too hungry to control herself, she sucked the blood from her fingers. She'd gone too long without feeding, a dangerous thing. Before she'd drank her fill, she noticed her family's crest on his armor. Quickly, Masie stood. Were there more men? If so, she wasn't safe.

Desperate to return to her sisters and warn them, a faint moan stopped her. She'd only made it a few feet, but had gone far enough to see dozens of men sprawled along the beach and well into the forest. She gasped. There were so many. Some groaned in agonizing pain, the others, not moving at all.

By the goddess... She ran back to her sisters.

"What is it?" Adaira asked with concern.

"There's...men...dead...on the shore. Come."

Adaira and Leana followed her.

"It looks like a battlefield," Adaira observed somberly.

"Aye. There's so much pain and death," Masie said, feeling their pain.

"We have no' eaten in days," Adaira said.

Masie whipped around and glared at her sister. "What are ye saying?"

"We'll end their suffering, Masie. In return, we'll be well fed."

Masie eyed the bodies. "They are suffering."

Adaira made the first move. Masie watched as her sister's eyes grew dark with bloodlust. White, sharp fangs extend from her mouth and she took a man by the neck and greedily fed upon him.

Leana did the same, consumed by a feeding frenzy.

This wasn't the first time they'd stumbled upon a battle. In fact, they preferred to feed on the fatally wounded. Unfortunately, choosing who was going to die always weighed heavy on Masie's heart.

She walked through the maze of men, pondering who would meet their maker when she heard a loud moan. An unexplainable feeling drove her toward the sound. The misery surrounded her, connecting her with the suffering man. *Maiden, mother, crone.* Was she too late?

"My angel of mercy." The gut-wrenching words stabbed Masie in the chest. It wasn't the first time she'd been called that.

She looked down, horrified by what she saw. He was lying in a pool of blood, his hand outstretched. "My angel," he wheezed as he struggled to breathe.

Masie kneeled next to him. "Please, conserve yer strength." Searching his body for the fatal wound, she moved his hands aside. Blood covered his ripped tunic. She found the deep gash. Sorrow shrouded her as she grieved for the loss of his life. A man she didn't know.

There was so much blood.

She ran her fingers through his sweaty, dark hair trying to provide some comfort.

"Please, mercy," he struggled to speak.

She brushed his cheek with the back of her hand. "I can end yer suffering." *But what a waste of life.* He was a warrior, strong and fearless. Masie imagined he had fought with that strength on the battlefield and deserved an honorable death.

Even through the sweat and blood, she sensed his

nobility. Aye, he was important. The gods had blessed him with superior looks--full lips and straight teeth.

Intrigued by her intuition, Masie admired his features more closely. Something shimmery caught her eye. The brooch pinned to his sash confirmed his birthright. Only a laird would wear such a jewel. Her hand trembled as she traced the black bird, well aware who wore the raven crest —her enemy.

Clan Gunn and Clan Keith had feuded for hundreds of years over territory, power, and trading rights. Dornoch and Wickshire land bordered the sea. Whoever ruled the sea, controlled the goods coming in and out of Caithness. Aye, the clans battled furiously and often.

But if he was the laird of Clan Gunn, why wasn't he wearing armor like the others?

"Please." The man swallowed hard, biting back the pain. "Angel, show me mercy."

Show him mercy? Why should she? He was the enemy. How many times did her people beg Clan Gunn for mercy and were denied? She should walk away and leave him to suffer, yet she couldn't. The hatred in her heart was for the queen.

She held his hand, offering comfort. She'd always wondered what the dying saw just before death. Rumors said it was a bright light calling you home. Yet, the rumor was just that. When she died, there was no light, only darkness and despair. Knowing firsthand how that misery felt, she could easily justify killing this man.

She bent down and whispered softly in his ear, "Close yer eyes and I'll end yer pain."

Masie tilted his head to the side, taking in his delicate flesh. An animalistic urge to feed flooded her veins and her fangs extended. She inhaled. Goddess, his scent was every bit masculine. Pine, sweat, and blood heightened the urge as she went in for the bite. She paused just before her teeth sank into his flesh. Something within his essence held her back. He had to live. She couldn't explain it, but she couldn't kill him. Aye, her heart was too big at times, or mayhap it was something more driving her. Whatever it was, she couldn't ignore it—she had to save this Highlander

Masie bit into her wrist and then tilted the man's head up. "Drink," she whispered. "Today is no' yer time to die."

With his Claymore held high, Kerr Gunn charged through the forest after the fleeing bastard. *Coward.* Even as he stood victorious in battle, he wasn't going to allow anyone to escape. Nay, he'd lost good men this eve and he'd avenge every last one of them until he drew his last breath.

He slashed his sword forward, slicing the enemy's back. The coward bellowed in pain and stumbled to the ground. Kerr kicked him over. The man grabbed Kerr's leg, slashing him with his dirk. Kerr growled. The fool still thought he had a chance.

Nothing pricked his arse more than allowing a rival clan to gain the upper hand. Kerr kicked the man in the ribs and stood over him. "May yer god have pity on yer soul," he snarled as he thrust his Claymore deep into the bastard's chest. Blood peppered Kerr's face. For good measure, or mayhap for pure pleasure, Kerr twisted the blade before he withdrew his weapon.

As of late, he'd grown unusually brutal, more times than he felt comfortable confessing. It was in his blood. He came from a strong and noble long line of Northmen. His ancestors sailed to Scotland, pillaging and defeating the

Pictish king for their small piece of Caithness. And he'd lay cold in the grave before he allowed anyone to take his rightful home.

With long purposeful strides, Kerr strode back through the woods to where he'd left his horse. He mounted and rode toward the loch. He had to find his brother. Last time he saw him, his brother was deep in battle. Clan Gunn remained victorious, but the blood bath had cost both clans dearly.

Kerr stopped as he approached three horses near the loch's edge. He didn't recognize the steeds. He proceeded with caution and dismounted, hoping to discover the strangers who owned the horses. He spied three women standing among the dead. Why were they on the battlefield? Were they thieves? Stripping the bodies of valuables? He crouched behind a thick tree trunk, planning his next move. He peeked out from the side of the tree, looking at the women, deciding which one would be easiest to catch. They were spread out, making his attack difficult.

Silently, he moved closer to the blonde with her back turned to him. A stag and white roses were embroidered on her cloak. Clan Keith. She was sitting next to his brother. *Shite!*

Something made a noise behind him and he spun around, careful that the blonde wouldn't see him. He prayed whatever had made the noise was either an animal or one of his men, for he didn't have time to waste, his brother needed help. Drawing his sword, he waited until whoever it was came closer. Three men wearing his clan's plaid crept out from the thick vegetation. Kerr signed in relief and sheathed his sword.

"Commander," Liam whispered in surprise. "We thought we lost ye."

"Nay, Liam, the devil is no' ready for me." Kerr smirked. "How many men do ye have?"

Liam cupped his hands to his mouth and cawed into the forest like a raven. Five men stood from their hiding places and made their way to their commander.

"Our laird is out there, injured," Kerr informed.

Liam unsheathed his sword and began to charge the battlefield. Kerr grabbed his arm, holding him back. "There's three women out there. One of them is with Bhaltair. I dinnae know who they are or why they are here. We must tread softly. If my gut is right, they could be spies from Clan Keith. We need all three captured. But above all else, we must get to my brother."

"Aye." Liam stood ready for command.

"Liam, take yer men and head toward the loch. Two of the women are there. The blonde is mine."

Liam nodded, signaling the plan into action.

Kerr grabbed his dirk from his boot and crept toward the tree line. He hoped for Bhaltair sake he wasn't too late.

When the time was right, Kerr snuck up behind the blonde and yanked her up by the hair. He pulled her against his body and pushed his blade into her neck. "Who are ye and what business do ye have here?"

"I'm no' a threat." The woman fought against his hold.

"No' a threat? Ye wear the Clan Keith stag."

"Let me go." The wind was knocked out of him as the lass elbowed him in the stomach. His grip loosened and she escaped.

Gasping for air, he still fought to gain the upper hand and ran after her. The wench was fast. He chased her to the loch. Lucky for him, she tripped once she hit the sandy shore, giving Kerr the perfect opportunity to catch her again. They tumbled to the ground.

"Get off me!"

He grabbed her fists as she pounded them against his chest. "Feisty, aye?"

"That man will die if ye dinnae let me go."

Kerr held her arms above her head. "What do ye mean he'll die?"

"His been fatally wounded. He needs a healer."

Suddenly, his attention was drawn to Liam and another warrior walking up from the loch with the other two women in their possession.

"Masie!" the raven-haired woman called out. "If ye hurt her, I will kill ye."

"Watch yer tongue, wench." Liam pushed her to the ground.

The lass ceased to fight. "Please, dinnae hurt my sisters. Let them go. Take me if ye must."

Kerr looked down into her pleading blue eyes, catching him off-guard. He'd never seen such a deep, vibrant color. They shimmered like sapphires. Fixated, a warm sensation surged through his body. A voice told him to let her go. What was going on?

Kerr shook his head, breaking eye contact with the lass and shaking free from the fog. His brows creased together as he glared down at her, unsure what had happened. He yanked the blonde to her feet as one of his men threw him a rope, then tied her hands behind her back.

An agonizing moan came from the forest. *Bhaltair!*

"Please, I can help him," the blonde beseeched.

"Why should I trust a Keith?" Kerr finished pulling the binds tight, then stepped back.

"Because he'll die if ye dinnae trust me."

Her gaze bore straight though him, causing his heart to skip a beat. For a brief moment, he wanted to believe her, but he never let his guard down, not even for a set of beautiful eyes.

"Liam, the dark-haired lass will ride with ye. Malcom, ye take the red-head. The blonde will ride with me," Kerr ordered. "Ye two." He pointed at two of his other men. "Make sure my bother makes it back home safely."

Kerr, took his prisoner by the arm, dragging her to his mount.

"Let me go, ye brute! Ye have no' right." She struggled against the restraints.

Kerr pushed the woman in front of him and grabbed her arms. "My gut tells me ye're a spy. And until I'm convinced otherwise, ye're my prisoner."

"Spy? I'm no' spy."

"We shall see, lassie." Kerr tugged her forward. He wrapped his big hands around her waist and lifted her onto his horse, then mounted behind her.

"Ye're making a big mistake."

"I'll be the judge of that," Kerr bit back as he kicked his steed into a gallop.

With each bounce, he was quickly reminded that he was sitting too close to lass. It was bad enough her arse was pressed against his cock, but why had he gone and tied her hands behind her back? Kerr looked between his legs. She'd grabbed the waist of his plaid to help keep balance.

Kerr fought back the unwanted thoughts of her hands wrapped around his manhood. He swallowed, reminding himself she was the sworn enemy. He wouldn't surrender to temptation or be bewitched by her beauty.

3

MASIE'S FOUGHT to keep her eyes open. They had traveled through the night, following the moonlit shoreline. The waves crashed onto the shore, distracting her from the horrid musings running through her mind about the barbarian sitting behind her. With her sisters captured as well, she refrained from doing anything to jeopardize their safety. The timing had to be right, then they would escape.

The sun will be out shortly. The morn was peeking over the horizon. She'd once before felt the sun's blistering rays, something she'd never do again. *Goddess*, she prayed they'd arrive soon to wherever they were going.

They rode up a steep cliff. A wall of jagged rock lie on one side, the raging ocean on the other. The horse stumbled, and out of pure reflex, Masie grabbed the nearest thing to brace herself—her captor's generous bollocks. Mortified at what she had done, she couldn't move a muscle. She heard him suck in a deep breath and felt his body tense.

Slowly, she removed her hands. "Lass, 'tis best ye keep yer hands to yerself. One false move and we're both over the cliff."

Too embarrassed to talk, Masie kept silent. Aye, she had already thought about grabbing ahold of his ballocks and twisting hard to get away. But she had to be smart and patient, like when they had escaped the fae queen. Being immortal, time was on her side as long as she could outrun the sun.

Finally, they reached flat ground and rode through a small settlement. Thatch-roofed cottages dotted the area. Folks paused from their daily chores and bowed as the contingent passed. With the loyalty these people displayed, Masie changed her mind about the men. They weren't a rouge band of brutes terrorizing young woman, but well respected warriors.

"Welcome to Raven's Landing." His hot breath on the back of her neck sent chills racing down her spine.

They crossed a bridge to the gatehouse where they were greeted by the stable hand. Masie was lifted from the horse and placed on her feet. Her legs threatened to buckle, numb from the long journey. Adaira and Leana were pushed into her.

"Masie, are ye well?" Adaira whispered.

"Aye." For the first time since she'd been captured, she'd felt a sense of relief. Together, she knew they would find a way out.

"Liam and Malcolm, take the prisoners to the north tower and wait for me." The man she'd been riding with glared at her. "Stay on guard."

"Aye." Liam grabbed Masie's binds and tugged her toward the tower, her sisters followed behind.

Masie stumbled up the winding stairs. Hunger had set in, which wasn't good for these humans. With the scent of blood coming from her captor's wound, her mouth watered and her fangs throbbed to sink into soft flesh.

Lust for blood was forgotten as the staircase opened into a spacious room. A hearth occupied one side of the wall, a table and chair positioned in front of it. Three doors were on the other wall.

"Red." Liam untied her sister's hands and then pushed her into one of the chambers and shut the door.

"Nay!" Masie cried out. "She no' to be alone."

"Hold yer tongue, Keith wench." Liam backhanded her.

Masie staggered, nearly falling down.

"Masie!" Adaira screamed.

Masie watched her sister struggle against Liam's grip as he freed her hands and pushed her into the next chamber. The door slammed shut causing Masie to shudder.

Liam now fixed his attention on Masie and licked his lips. She took a step back, shaking her head. "Please, dinnae touch me."

Liam stalked up to her and grabbed a fistful of her hair, yanking her head back. "I'll do what I want wit' ye."

The ale on his breath turned her stomach. She glared into his eyes. "Do what ye will wit' me. Make it fast, for the second ye're no' watching, I'll kill ye."

"Och, I'll have my pleasure fucking the feisty right out of ye." Liam untied his trews.

"Liam!" A strong voice commanded from the stairs, causing the guard to take pause. "I said to guard the prisoners, no' fuck them. Please excuse his behavior. Enemy or no', Clan Gunn does no' abuse woman."

Liam released her, cutting the ropes from her hands and then stalked away. Rubbing her wrists, Masie glowered at the man who had saved her. "Och, 'tis debatable."

The grim expression on his face told her he wasn't looking to argue.

"Ye said ye could help my brother. Are ye a healer?"

Masie didn't know how to answer his question. Aye, she had a keen knowledge of herbs, but she was far from being a true healer. "Aye."

"Come wit' me."

Masie pulled her arm from his grip. "Why should I? Ye tied me up as if I'm a criminal and now ye want my help? Besides, I dinnae know yer name."

"I'm Kerr Gunn. Bhaltair is my brother and laird. Please, I can no' lose him." The sorrow showed through his rough exterior.

Masie hesitated. Her good sense told her to deny his request. Yet, she still couldn't shake the feeling she had to help his brother. "I want something in return."

"If ye ask me to let ye go, I can no'."

"Then I ask ye to keep that bastard away from me and my sisters." Masie folded her arms across her chest, still feeling violated from Liam's attack.

"Aye. Ye have my word."

"Then I shall see to yer brother."

The bedchamber was dark, yet Masie had no problem seeing the bed draped in blue and green silks. A candle flickered on a table next to the bed. Masie approached the laird. He was wrapped in a fur, sweat glistened on his pale skin.

"I'm afraid he's mortally wounded," Kerr said from behind her.

Masie felt the love Kerr had for his brother and the sorrow. It ran deep. She could relate. The journey her sisters had endured with the queen was full of misery. Disobeying the queen came with grave consequences—ones that scarred her soul forever. The haunting sound of a whip cracking, the sting of a leather strap slicing through flesh, these things were meant to never heal.

Aye, she would save the laird but with caution. "I will do whatever I can to help him but his injury is verra bad. I'll need some items."

"Anything."

"I'll need warm water, cloth, and wolfbane for the pain."

"Aye. Anything else?"

"It wouldn't hurt to pray."

As he left the chamber, Masie quickly pulled the furs back from the injured man. She didn't need those supplies to heal him, what she did need was time alone with him. She couldn't have the man drinking from her wrist in front of an audience.

She ripped the tunic from his body to examine the wound. It had started to heal from the blood she'd already given him. She felt his forehead, he was burning up with fever.

She extended her fangs and sliced her wrist, then held it to his lips. "Drink for me."

Masie felt him suck harder and harder. She threaded her fingers through his dark head of curls, soothing him as he drank. Keeping her eye on the door, she knew Kerr would be back soon and wouldn't risk getting caught. She just hoped the wound wouldn't heal by the time he returned, for she'd be found out.

Masie pulled her wrist away and licked the cut. The gash sealed instantly. As the man fell back to unconsciousness, she removed the rest of his tunic. The door flew open and Kerr strode in holding a bowl of water and a handful of cloths.

"Just in time," Masie said. "Lay them on the bed."

With haste, she wetted a cloth and washed away the blood from the wound. Even with her blood, it was still very deep and painful. She carefully wrapped a bandage around his stomach, covering the wound.

She wet another cloth and placed it on his forehead.

"My angel of mercy," Bhaltair murmured.

"Shh, rest."

"Please, do no' leave me. I can no' die alone."

His words went straight to Masie's heart. "This day is no' yer time. Yer brother is here."

"Kerr." He reached out and his brother caught his flailing hand.

"I'm here, Brother."

"I dinnae want to fall asleep, for I fear I will no' wake." He swallowed shallowly. "Sing to me, tell a story, anything, but dinnae allow me to sleep."

Masie glanced at Kerr. He nodded, motioning her to grant his brother's request. Nervously, she thought of something to say. She couldn't sing. Leana had that gift. She did remember a story her mother once told her about a Greek goddess.

Masie cleared her throat. "Are ye familiar wit' the goddess, Aphrodite?"

"Nay," he struggled to talk.

"Och. Aphrodite is the captivating Greek goddess of love, beauty, and marriage. They say she rose from the foam of the raging seas and her beauty was beyond compare. People from all over the world came to her shores to bathe. One day, she fell in love wit' a mortal man, Adonis. He was strong, handsome, and liked to hunt. While out on a hunt, Adonis battled wit' a wild boar. The beastie was too powerful. In one fatal thrust, the boar swung his head into Adonis, impaling his ballocks with his tusk."

Masie glared at Kerr.

"Once word reached Aphrodite, she climbed into her swan-drawn chariot and rushed into the forest, searching for her beloved Adonis. Dread and despair ripped through her as she saw Adonis lying in a bloody heap on the ground. She picked him up, cradling him to her breasts. As she carried him back to her chariot, blood trailed behind him. Every spring, it is said mysterious red flowers bloom throughout the forest. People believe it's Adonis coming back to life to reunite with Aphrodite."

"That's the daftest thing I've heard, lass," Kerr said as he looked at Masie as if she'd grown two-heads.

"'Tis no'." She stood with her hands on her hips.

"A chariot drawn by swans? A woman made from sea foam? She sounds more like a sea hag," Kerr grumbled.

"Obviously, ye're too blind to see the true meaning of the story," Masie huffed.

"And what may that be? Never fall in love wit'a bonny lass? I dinnae have that problem."

"Nay, 'tis about life, death, and rebirth. And love, in which ye apparently know nothing about."

Kerr stood and grabbed her arm, pulling her close. He towered over her. "I dinnae love. I fuck and slay. 'Tis what I do."

Masie shuddered from the intensity pouring off him. She had no doubt he meant every word he said.

With her body so close to his, she could feel the lean muscles of his chest through his tunic. The hard lines under his eyes declared he'd hadn't sleep in days. A thick vein ran down his neck and disappeared under his tunic. She swallowed back the temptation to extend her fangs and bite into his tender flesh. Indeed, biting him would quench her hunger. More than anything else, the urge to put him in his place weighed heavier. No one had ever provoked her like this, not even the fae queen. He ignited an anger inside her she hadn't known existed.

"The lass is right, Kerr." His brother chuckled. "Ye dinnae have a loving bone in yer body."

Kerr snapped his attention to his brother.

"'Tis true," Bhaltair said.

"Since when is my lack of affection the center of discussion?"

"All I'm saying is it wouldn't hurt to show a wee bit of compassion."

Masie snickered.

"Lass, yer job here is done." He grabbed her arm and forced her through the bedchamber door.

All the way back to the tower, Masie had to run to keep up with Kerr. Apparently, his brother struck a nerve and he was taking it out on her. She prayed he would keep his word and not hurt her or her sisters.

He swung the chamber door open and walked Masie inside.

"Someone will fetch ye in the morn."

"Please, I've done nothing wrong."

He ignored her plea and locked her in.

Masie ran to door, bagging her fist on it. "Ye can no' keep me in here," she yelled.

When he didn't reply, she spun around, taking in the small space. A cot took up one side of the room and a stone wall separated her from Adaira.

Masie called out, "Adaira!"

She didn't reply.

"Please." Tears streamed down her face. "I dinnae want to be alone." She pulled her hands through her hair and spun around. It was getting hard to breathe.

In all her life, she'd never been separated from her sisters like this. She had to find a way out. The brute-of-a-man had no right to treat them like criminals. For the love of goddess, she'd just saved the laird.

Masie took a fur from the cot and laid it down on the floor next to the wall separating her from Adaira. She curled herself into a ball, wrapping her cloak around her shivering body. She closed her eyes tight and thought of Adaira. *Can ye hear me, Sister?* She strained to communicate through mind-speak. It wasn't long before exhaustion took over and she fell asleep.

4

LAIRD CORMAG WATCHED as the vessel carrying his dead son's body floated out to sea. Hard lines creased his face but he didn't shed a tear. It wasn't because he didn't love his son. If he succumbed to the pain of losing his only child, it would be the death of him. Beathan Keith had a bright future.

Cormag thought the curse had ended with Helen's death, but watching his son sail into the horizon awakened the demons he'd put to rest years ago. Aye, Helen's curse on Dornoch was very much alive.

Everything about that woman irked him. He'd warned Doughall not to take another man's wife—it came with grave consequences. But his words fell on deaf ears. It was impossible to get anything through his thick skull. The wench had driven an honorable man to madness and failed to give Doughall an heir. This was just the beginning. If his assumptions were right, Helen had seen a healer and took herbs to ensure she'd never have a son, further cursing the clan.

After her death, his comrade's condition worsened.

Plagued by visions of a dark fairy who came to him at night, Cormag had found Doughall on numerous occasions aimlessly walking the battlements and muttering to himself. It broke his heart witnessing his friend's downfall, weakened to a shell of a man. But knowing there wasn't a damn thing he could do to stop it hurt the most.

Cormag gritted his teeth and balled his fists in anger. Out of respect for Doughall, he'd welcomed his daughters back to Dornoch Castle. And this was their way of showing gratitude, by killing his only son?

Nay, the curse will end.

A cold wind chilled him to the bone as he gathered his cloak closer to his body. He nodded to the archers waiting with their fiery arrows, indicating it was time to set the funeral ship afire. Five arrows streaked through the air, lighting up the gray sky. A deep gloom set in as he watched the vessel ignite.

As long as the Keith daughters were still alive he'd be cursed, his clan would live under constant threat, and his seat as Laird Keith would be jeopardized. He vowed to avenge his son. There was no doubt these girls were behind his son's murder. Ever since the wenches returned things seemed amiss. They were different. He sensed evil and he should have put an end to it long ago. Bloody witches!

An image of Beathen flashed before him, pale and drained of all his blood. No normal beast or man would have been able to desecrate his body. It had to be the devil's work. They'd burn for their sins. They'd burn to end the curse. They'd burn for his son.

"My laird." A man stood next to him with his hand on the hilt of his sword. "Excuse the interruption. News has reached me about Doughall's daughters."

Cormag stared ahead as the flames disappeared over the

horizon. "'Tis no' the time, Hamish. I'm sending my son to God."

"Aye. Please accept my deepest sympathy." Hamish bowed. "But I have news that would interest ye."

Cormag raised a black brow. "Continue."

"My scout has spotted the Keith sisters," Hamish informed. "They've been seen riding with Clan Gunn north."

"How long ago?" the laird asked.

"Two days."

Bile rose in the back of his throat. Treasonous wenches. All along they'd been plotting against their own clan. Did they think joining the enemy would secure their birthright to the Clan Keith seat? *Nay, the wenches would hang.*

"Send word to Laird Gunn. He's to return the girls for questioning regarding my son's death. I dinnae want a war. I want justice."

5

A SLIVER of sunlight beamed through Masie's chamber causing her to wake. She sat up, quickly moving into the shadows. She felt weak from the lack of blood and must conserve what little energy she had left.

"Masie." She heard her name faintly in her mind.

"Adaira?"

"Aye."

"Oh, thank the gods! Are ye well?"

"I'm well."

"How's Leana?"

"I can no' reach her."

"The laird's brother has promised us protection for what it's worth."

"His word means nothing to me. Masie, I promise ye, I will get us out of here."

"I know."

Her chamber door cracked open and Masie slowly stood, pressing her body against the clod stone wall, away from the sunlight. She searched the room for anything that could be used as a weapon. Unfortunately, she didn't even have a chamber pot to throw at the intruder.

A man slipped in. "Commander Kerr has sent me to fetch ye and yer sisters. 'Tis time to break yer fast."

"Ye can tell yer commander I'm no'..." Masie paused as a thought dawned on her. This was her chance to escape. She'd obey and find a way out.

Masie stepped out of the darkness. She eyed the man's neck and smiled. "I'm famished." Masie placed her hands in front of her, offering them peacefully to the man.

Cautiously, he tied a rope around her wrists, then pushed her out the door. Masie beamed as she saw Adaira and Leana waiting. Their hands were tied, too. He pushed Masie into Adaira. "Move, wench."

Masie stumbled into her sister. "Adaira."

"Aye." Adaira gave her a knowing glance, telling her everything would be all right.

"Hold yer tongue," the man spat, pushing the girls down the stairs.

Once inside the great hall, the massive room came alive. Trenchers banged together as people ate and chattered. Everyone was enjoying the company around them like one big family. Inside, Masie sighed, for she'd always wished for a family like this. Something slammed into her, almost knocking her over. A boy no older than five looked up at her. "Och, laddie, ye should watch where ye're going." Masie smiled.

"Edmund, come here." His mother pulled the wee boy away, glaring at Masie as if she was the devil's daughter. The woman and child scurried back to their table.

Her rope was tugged and she stumbled forward. The guard stopped at an empty table close to the kitchens and released her hands. Leana slid down the bench and Adaira followed. "Dinnea try anything daft. I'll be watching ye," the man warned.

Masie looked at Leana. She hadn't been the same since that dreadful night. "Leana," Masie whispered.

Her sister slowly turned.

"Are ye well, lass? Has anyone hurt ye?"

She shook her head.

Relief washed over her. She'd feared the worst, like Liam having his way with Leana.

"Something is amiss here," Adaira said.

Aye, Masie felt it as soon as she walked in the hall. She could feel the clan's scrutinizing glares. They knew they were the enemy.

"They're no' treating us like prisoners," Masie said. "Prisoners are kept in the dungeon and no' allowed to eat wit' the clan."

"Aye, something is verra strange."

A plump woman appeared and slammed a bowl of soup down in front of Masie. Oats spilled over the side. The aroma turned her stomach.

"'Tis all we have left." The woman did the same to Adaira, then returned to the kitchen.

Masie pushed the gruel away.

"Masie, we have to try and fit in if we have any chance of escaping," Adaira said.

"I will no' eat this. I need something more."

"I know, but we can no' take unnecessary risks."

Masie pulled the bowl in front of her and stared into the watery oats. She picked up her spoon and began to eat when she overheard two women talking two tables up. Normally, she could control the sensitivity of her hearing, but she was too weak. She could hear them as if they were talking in her head.

"I heard the Keith girls are witches," said one woman.

"Aye, I can no' believe Kerr would bring such sin into our clan." The woman looked over her shoulder at Masie.

One was very young, perhaps of marrying age. Her light-brown hair hung past her waist and was twisted into a long braid. Her dress was dark blue and made from velvet. A noblewoman, Masie thought.

The lass sitting next to the brunette grabbed her arm, bringing the woman's attention to her, "Dinnae stare long. Ye'll turn to stone." The women laughed.

Anger streaked up Masie's spine. How dare they judge her and her sisters. God's bones, she'd risked everything by healing the laird. She wasn't a monster. The more she heard their callous laughter the more her hunger for blood surfaced. She set her eyes on the soft flesh behind the brunette's ear. Before she knew what was happening, Masie's fangs extended.

"Masie," Adaira said, astonished by her sister's actions. "Are ye mad?"

Masie shook free from her wicked thoughts and clamped her hand over her mouth when she realized what she had just done.

"Eat the gruel, Masie, and dinnae cause a scene," Adaira warned.

Masie dismissed the urge to rip through the woman's throat, but the anger was still there. She wasn't going to allow such rumors to be spread so easily.

Masie stood.

"Masie, please sit down." Adaira pulled on her arm.

"I can no' allow some simple-minded eejit to get away wit' spreading lies about us, Adaira." She yanked free and ran her hands down the front of her dress, smoothing out the material as she strode over to the table.

The women looked at her wide-eyed as Masie stood in front of them with her hands planted on the table. She gazed at the blonde who looked scared enough to wet herself.

"Ye know what I heard?" Masie asked.

The brunette shook her head slowly.

"I heard if ye look deep into their eyes, ye'll see yer true soul staring back at ye." Suddenly, Masie's long, blonde hair changed into white, straggly strands, her face transformed into a wrinkled mask, and her hands changed into hooves.

Startled, the women leaned back and held their mouths to stifle their screams.

Satisfied she's shut them up, Masie shook her head and retuned back to normal, leaving the women speechless.

"Ye should be careful who ye mock and spread rumors about." Masie smirked.

Masie made her way back to her sisters. Adaira scowled at her.

"I told ye no' to cause a scene."

"I know, but—"

"'Tis time to get to work." The same man who fetched them interrupted.

"I do no' understand," Masie questioned. "I need to see to the laird. I need to speak with Commander Kerr."

"Ye'll do as I say," The man exclaimed.

He bound their wrists again and tugged them into the kitchen. "Miss Sinclair, these are commander Kerr's prisoners and are to be put to work."

"Aye." The plump cook eyed the girls. "It be my pleasure to show the lassies my kitchen."

Masie looked around, trenchers were piled high, the kettle in the center of the room hanging over an open fire was plastered with oatmeal and flies were swarming a barrel with who knew what was inside.

"Fair one." The cook pointed to Masie. "Ye scrub the cauldron. I believe ye're familiar wit' it," she snickered.

"The rest of ye wash the trenchers. I need to prepare for the evening meal." The cook waddled to a basket full of vegetables and began to clean and chop them.

Masie glared at the cook as she walked away. The gruel inside bubbled and popped. She wrinkled her nose. This was absurd. She didn't deserve to be treated like a servant, much less, a prisoner.

The rest of the morn and well into the late afternoon, Masie tackled the black beast. She scrubbed, scraped, and vowed to never look at gruel again. After the kettle was clean, Miss Sinclair had ordered her to ready a fire for the evening meal. Masie shoveled the old ash out and replaced it with fresh wood. She needed more kindling.

"Miss Sinclair, we need more wood," Masie informed the cook.

"Then go fetch it child. I'm busy."

Masie saw an empty space in the corner where one piece of wood sat. "There's only one piece left."

The cook waved her off.

Not sure of her boundaries, Masie carefully opened the back door. To her relief, the sun was nowhere to be seen. Feather-light snow flakes fluttered from the sky, covering the ground in white.

"Dinnae try anything sneaky," The cook called out. "Clan Gunn has eyes everywhere."

Masie closed the door, thankful to be rid of Sinclair even if it was for a short time. She walked over to a woodshed, open in the front. "Of course there's no wood." She stood with her hands on her hips.

A stump and large chunks of wood were scattered on the ground next to the shed, as if someone had forgotten their chore. Frustrated, Masie picked up a chuck of wood and set it up on the stump. She grabbed the axe and wished a certain someone was around so she could tell him how she felt. She wasn't a servant.

She lifted the axe over her head, letting all her anger and frustration out. Slamming the axe down, it splintering the wood. She repeated the effort. Not knowing her own strength, on the last strike, she embedded the blade deep in the stump. She pulled and pulled on the handle trying to get it out, but it didn't budge.

"Shite."

She tried again, the damn thing was stuck. Frustrated, Masie picked up the hunks of wood and began to walk back to the kitchen. She stopped abruptly. Off in the distance, her attention was drawn to swords clanging together. Curious, she dropped the wood in the snow and followed the sound.

Inside the bailey, a man was training a lad to wield a sword. As she got closer and realized who the man was, all the pent-up anger came rushing back. It was Kerr.

Masie leaned her back against a tree and crossed her arms over her chest as she watched him swing his weapon through the air. She wasn't leaving until she voiced her opinion. He had no right in keeping her here without cause. She needed to find a way to convince the laird to let them go. Masie studied him. There was no denying it, the man was a true warrior, carved by the god of war himself. He swung his sword, demanding the lad to fight back. Pure, raw strength radiated off him. He was firm with the lad, yet showed immense tolerance.

Kerr looked up, noticing her watching him. Their gazes locked for a moment and Masie's cheeks heated. Caught by a wave of surprising desire, it felt as if she was drowning in his smoldering glare. Why was her body betraying her? With one look, Masie lost her will to fight. This man had taken her prisoner. She wanted to rip him limb-from-limb, but at the same time, he lit a flame deep inside her. A feeling she had no experience with.

"Laddie, always keep ye eyes on the enemy," Kerr instructed as he watched Masie.

Masie couldn't contain her laughter when the lad took advantage of Kerr's distracted state and kicked him in the shin.

Surprised, Kerr dropped his sword and grabbed his leg. "Verra good, lad."

Masie chuckled and wished it had been her doing the kicking.

Kerr retrieved his sword and rustled the lad's hair. "We'll work on yer stance tomorrow. I have business to attend to."

The lad smiled. "Ye promise?"

"Och, ye question my word?" He playfully placed his hand over his heart.

"Nay." The lad grinned and ran toward the armory.

Kerr began to walk in the opposite direction, which told her he was avoiding her. Masie ran after him.

"He looks like ye," Masie said.

Kerr whipped around and she almost bumped into him. "Who?"

"The lad. He's yer son, aye?"

"Nephew."

"His mum must be verra proud."

"Aye, she would have been if she was still alive."

"I'm so sorry."

"My sister was a fine woman. She died during childbirth. Her husband drank himself to death afterward. Being

Rabbie's guardian is the best thing that has ever happened to me."

"A child is a parent's greatest accomplishment. Her memory will live on in him."

"Aye." Kerr exhaled and quickly changed the subject. "Why are ye here? Shouldn't ye be in the kitchen with Sinclair?"

Appalled, Masie said, "It was ye who put me and my sisters on kitchen duty?"

"Would ye rather me put ye in dungeon wit' the other prisoners?"

"Nay," she bit back. "I want to speak to the laird."

"Nay." Kerr walked past her, heading to the castle.

"How long are ye going to keep us here?"

Kerr turned around and gave her a sideways glance. "As long as I wish."

"'Tis no' right."

"Nothing is right during wartime." She flinched when he wiped a smudge of soot from her cheek.

Masie's heart skipped a beat. She didn't like the way her body reacted to his touch. "I have done nothing wrong. If I was a spy why would I have helped yer brother?"

Kerr studied her for a moment, longer than she felt comfortable with. She cleared her throat. "I demand to speak to the laird."

"Aye, Kerr, why have ye kept me from my angel of mercy?"

"Bhaltair," Kerr said, surprised to see his brother out of bed. "Ye should be resting."

"Brother, I feel well, there's no need for me to stay cooped up."

"Laird Gunn, yer brother is right, ye should rest. Ye've suffered a great injury," Masie added.

"Och, lass, 'tis ye I want to see." He pulled his fur-lined coat up on his shoulders. "I hope my brother has been hospitable and welcomed ye to our clan."

Masie paused. He clearly had no idea what Kerr had done.

"Bhaltair, she's a Keith. We found her and her sisters on the battlefield. They could be spies."

Masie planted her hands on her hips. "I'm no spy."

"Spies?" Bhaltair exclaimed. "Why were ye on the battlefield, lass, if yer no' a spy?"

Masie had to decide how much to tell him. She couldn't reveal she'd fled home because her sister murdered two men, nor that they were feeding on human blood. "I can no' say, but I can assure ye, I'm no' a spy."

"I can no' let ye leave without knowing why. Surely ye must understand my concerns," Bhaltair said.

Masie stood in front of the laird and took his hand, looking deep into his eyes, honing in on his vulnerability, which was saying no to a beautiful lass. "If I was a spy, would I have healed ye?" Influencing a human's mind was something she did sparingly.

"Nay," Bhaltair replied as if he was in a trace.

"It would be in your best interest to let us go."

"Aye."

She had him right where she wanted him. Her sisters would be on horseback by nightfall.

"By the gods, Bhaltair!" Kerr interrupted, pulling his brother from the daze. "Yer inability to tame yer cock around a beautiful woman is a disgrace."

Masie's heart dove into her stomach in defeat.

Bhaltair shook his head. "What?"

"Ye're no' going to let them go without further investigation are ye?" Kerr exclaimed.

"Nay," Bhaltair cleared his throat. "Of course not."

"Brother?" Kerr eyed him with concern. "Are ye well? I think ye should rest."

"Aye," Masie intervened. "I'll take ye back to yer bedchamber. I should take a look at yer bandage."

"Dinnae fash yerself. I feel well," the laird grumbled.

"Dinnae be stubborn. I'm worried about infection." She batted her eyelashes a few times to drive the stake right through his heart. Bhaltair seemed to be the reasonable one. Mayhap, if she was alone with him, she could convince him she wasn't a spy.

"Och, Miss—"

"Masie," she replied.

"Miss Masie, if it will appease ye, then I will allow it." Bhaltair offered his arm and she accepted, wrapping her hand around his bicep. They made their way to the castle.

He leaned in and whispered in her ear. "Lass, ye're quite charming."

Masie giggled. Aye, she was.

"Masie, I hope ye find our clan is hospitable."

"Actually..." She glared back at Kerr who looked dumfound that a lass had bested him. "If yer idea of hospitable is keeping me locked up in a small room without my sisters and treating us as servants, than nay, I find yer ways distasteful."

"Where is Kerr keeping ye? Better no' be in the dungeons."

"In a tower." Masie pointed to the north tower.

"The north tower!" Bhaltair shoved his hand through his curly hair. He looked at Masie. "I be verra sorry for my brother's behavior."

They reached the great hall and walked upstairs to

Bhaltair's bedchamber. "Here." She pointed to the bed. "Sit down and take off yer tunic."

Bhaltair's sly grin didn't go unnoticed. Masie took his cloak and tunic and laid them next to him. She went to look at the bandage and her heart stopped. *On no!* The laird was lying back, resting on his elbows with a sly grin on his face.

"No' too many lasses make it up to my bedchamber." He looked up at her and winked.

She was afraid this would happen. Her blood had the power to heal but it also enhanced sexual desires. Bhaltair was experiencing intense infatuation which in time would go away, however, she had given him a lot of blood. *Maiden, mother, crone.* What was she going to do? She had already tried using her charm which only made it worse. And she was not giving up her virginity that easily. Bedding the laird to make a deal—nay, that was a bold move she'd never make.

"Come." He patted the bed. "Sit wit' me." "I'm no' a lass wishing to bed the laird. I'm only here to tend to yer wound." She began removing the bandage.

"I would like a chance to repay my debt to ye for saving me," he said as he threaded a strand of her hair through his fingers.

"I think I've been verra clear, my laird, yer debt will be paid if ye let us go."

"Aye, ye have, but ye must understand my position. Until I know why ye were on the battlefield, I forbid ye to leave. Until then, ye are guests and I will see to it personally ye're moved to the main tower. Ye're welcome in my bedchamber. In fact, I encourage it." He flashed her a smile.

Not accustomed to such advances, she sensed she needed to get out before Bhaltair did something horrible.

"Laird—"

"Bhaltair."

"Bhaltair, ye too think I'm a spy"

"I must know the facts, lass. My clan's safety comes first." He sat up and looked down at his stomach. "God's teeth, 'tis healed, completely." He looked at Masie, bewildered. "Ye gift of healing is unlike any I've ever seen."

"Aye. Using the proper herbs makes all the difference," Masie lied, hoping he would believe her.

Bhaltair stood and took Masie's hands, examining them like they were jewels. Unlike his brother, he had a gentler nature. "These hands are magic."

"Bhaltair, I must go." He dipped his head—goddess, he was going to kiss her. "The herbs are clouding yer judgment." She could barely get the words out. Panicked, she tried to pull away, but he tightened his grip.

"Lass." He tipped her chin up so she had to look at him. "Who are ye?" His lips brushed over hers.

"Pardon me." A familiar voice she'd grown to know came from the door. *Kerr.*

Guilt consumed her. Why was she feeling this way? He had no claim on her, yet the heat of Kerr's gaze told her differently, like she'd been caught doing something wrong. She stepped back, breaking Bhaltair's hold. "Excuse me, I was just leaving." She began to walk away.

"Nay." Bhaltair grabbed her arm, stopping her. "Kerr, see to it that Masie and her sisters are moved from the north tower to guest quarters."

"Guests?" Kerr exclaimed.

"Aye, until we settle our differences, the Keith girls are welcome in our clan."

Kerr scowled. "Ye're making a big mistake."

"So be it."

6

AFTER HOURS of walking off his anger, Kerr found himself in the solar, deep in ale, and hopefully soon to pass out. How could his brother chastise him in front of Masie? Moreover, the laird wasn't using good judgment. He was thinking with his cock.

Kerr didn't regret locking the girls in the tower. He'd done what he thought was right, protect his brother and their land. After hundreds of years of feuding, the hatred toward the Keith's flowed through his blood like a river. It ran soul-deep. How could Bhaltair be so quick to dismiss the Keith girls? They could very well be spies. In fact, given the chance, Masie didn't explain herself. Wasn't that a sign of guilt?

Kerr poured himself more ale and sat heavily in a chair in front of the hearth. He glowered into the flames as he took a long pull from his tankard.

Masie. Aye, he'd never seen beauty quite like hers before. Her creamy skin was flawless. High cheek bones, pert nose, her voice as sweet as a bird's song. But, what made his cock hard, was the way she showed no fear. She had a stubborn streak he could relate to.

Sweet wee lass, move along, ye will no' affect me.

Kerr threw his empty tankard into the fire as he succumbed to the ale. He wasn't the kind to take a wife. His demons were his only friends and, of late, even they were turning on him. The battlefield was the only place for him and all he had room for in his heart. Long ago, his father had warned him a man had to pay for the wickedness he'd done. Aye, he'd pay.

He would not allow a lass to plague his thoughts like his father had done. A broken heart was the death of a man. It showed weakness and he was far from it. A warrior, he'd die before allowing anything to harm his clan or the ones he loved. Because he was Bhaltair's closest adviser, it was his responsibility to protect the laird from outside influences. Especially a beautiful lass.

Kerr's mind swam in a drunken fog. Feeling the warmth from the ale and fire, he needed some cool air. He stood and staggered to the arched window next to the hearth overlooking the main tower where their guests stayed. He breathed in the cold winter air, feeling the chill all over his body.

Aye, he could see it on Bhaltair's face, he'd been bewitched.

Something moved in the window across from his. He squinted—was it a person? Aye. A female. The moonlight illumined the silhouette giving him a glorious view, for she was naked. He leaned back and enjoyed as the woman swayed seductively, brushing her hair. His gaze roamed her body, from her flared hips up to her full breasts. He had to see who this mysterious lass was. As he looked up at her face, he was left speechless.

Masie? Naked?

He straightened. He should turn away and give her privacy. But he couldn't tear his eyes off her. Her creamy flesh beckoned him, made him want to do things to her that would make the devil blush.

Brushing her hair in long stokes, it fell attractively over her breasts. What he'd give to shove his hands through those silken strands while he kissed her red lips until he left her breathless. As if he needed more reasons to want her, she gathered her hair, draping it over one shoulder, revealing full round breasts. Kerr licked his lips. He should close the fur over the window but he was in too deep.

His eyes roamed further down her flat stomach. Her skin was white and smooth. Sucking in a shaky breath, his gaze settled betwixt her legs where a patch of blonde curls hid her womanhood. He adjusted himself as his cock strained against his trews.

A growl escaped his lips. He'd never wanted a woman like he wanted Masie right now. She'd cast a powerful spell on him and he couldn't fight the attraction.

Swallowing hard, he followed her hand as she caressed between her breasts and up her neck. By the saints, this lass set him on fire. Their eyes met and he watched her red lips spread into a wicked grin. She knew he was watching and didn't once try to stop it. Should he go to her?

"Shite." He dragged himself away from the window. The urge to go to Masie pulled him toward the solar door. He paused before he opened it. *What are ye doing? She's the enemy.*

As soon as Masie felt his smoldering gaze upon her body,

she couldn't resist the urge to stand in the moonlight, allowing Kerr to watch her. She should have pulled the furs over the window, but this was too much fun. He intrigued her. She liked the excitement, knowing he could look but not touch. Mayhap she should use it to her advantage to escape.

Unfortunately, her heart told her differently.

When Kerr didn't return to the window, Masie couldn't help but think about him coming to her door. She hadn't been with a man before. Kerr brought all her lustful thoughts to the surface. It made no sense. He hated her and, quite frankly, the feelings were mutual.

A knock at the door startled her. Was it Kerr? Quickly, she donned her shift and robe. She cracked open the door and peeked out.

"Masie, 'tis me, Adaira. Let me in."

Relieved and perhaps a wee bit disappointed, she let her sister in.

"Where's Leana?" Masie asked.

"Asleep." Adaira looked around the bedchamber. "Och, ye have yer own room?"

Masie's brows creased together. "I thought we all had separate rooms."

"Nay. Are ye going to tell me what's going on?" Adaira planted her hands on her hips. "Ye never came back to the kitchen, then Leana and I were escorted to a beautiful bedchamber with clean clothes and a warm bath waiting for us."

Masie sat down on the edge of the bed. "Dinnae be angry wit' me." Masie looked down into her lap. "I saved the laird."

Adaira stood astounded. "Ye did what?"

"I could no' let him die. Laird Gunn has promised to see to our every need."

"Did he promise to let us go?"

Masie sat quietly, still avoiding eye contact.

"Masie."

"He will no' let us go until he's convinced we're no' spies."

"What did ye tell him?"

"Adaira, I swear on Mum's grave, I didnae tell him anything. Bhaltair and his brother Kerr know nothing about who we are or why we were on the battlefield. That's why we're still here."

Adaira sat down next Masie and put her arm around her. "Since we are free to walk about the clan, tomorrow I'll find a way to escape."

"Mayhap we should stay," Masie said nervously.

"Are ye daft?"

"Nay, Cormag wouldn't think to search for us here. And if he did, why would he care if we're in the enemy's hands?"

"Masie, Cormag will no' stop hunting us until justice is served. The longer we stay, we become a threat to these people. We must leave."

"Aye, I understand," Masie agreed and hugged her sister tightly. "Can I sleep wit' Leana and ye tonight?"

Adaira smiled. "Of course."

"I'll be right over. I need to grab a few things," Masie said.

"Fine. The door will be open." Adaira quit the bedchamber.

Masie sighed. She knew her sister was right. Cormag would destroy Wickshire looking for them. She couldn't allow harm to fall on these innocent people, enemy or naught. They couldn't stay.

But still, she couldn't shake the disappointment forming in her heart. She'd never know what it would feel like to be loved by Kerr. She grabbed her cloak. This was absurd, lusting over a man who had the grace of a barbarian, a said enemy. Leaving as soon as possible was best before she wound up knee-deep in trouble. And Kerr was definitely trouble.

7

"KERR, WAKE UP YE LOUT." Bhaltair shoved his brother who was slouched over in the chair. "Ye missed breaking yer fast."

Bhaltair walked over to the small table in front of the hearth and placed a few hunks of bread wrapped in a cloth down. He picked up the empty pitcher of ale lying on its side. "I see ye had company last night."

Kerr groaned. His head pounded.

"I met the rest of the Keith girls this morn while breaking my fast with Masie. Verra lovely lasses."

An image of Masie's naked body flashed through Kerr's foggy mind. Did he actually go to her? Aye, he remembered, but she didn't come to the door. And by the way his ballocks were still throbbing, nothing had happened between them. He must have returned to the solar and passed out. "Ye saw Masie this morn?" Kerr sat up slowly.

"Aye. I'm escorting her to the village square. I'm hopeful to gain her trust and find out her wee secret. Do ye want to join us."

Nay! His first response failed his lips. "Aye."

Bhaltair smiled. "Good. May the best man win her affection."

"And what is that supposed to mean?" Kerr rubbed his temples.

If he wanted to challenge him, there were many other reasons than over a woman. Growing up, Bhaltair never wavered in his attempt to best him every chance he got. When Kerr was finally old enough and strong enough, he'd put up a good fight, showing he wasn't scared of Bhaltair.

"I see the way ye look at her." Bhaltair wiggled his brows. "She's a fine lass."

"Brother, I dinnae want a lass. I dinnae want forever," Kerr grumbled.

"It wouldn't hurt ye to open yer heart."

Kerr stood. "I dinna remember asking ye for advice about women. Furthermore, if ye like her so much, then take her for a wife. Nothing is standing in yer way. Except she's a Keith. Now, if ye'll excuse me, I need to wash before we leave."

Bhaltair shook his head. "Yer as stubborn as Da."

Kerr waved Bhaltair off as he left the solar.

Masie blushed as soon as Kerr strode into the stables. Her heart was beating so fast it was going to leap from her chest. As soon as their eyes met, Masie could feel her temperature rise.

He nodded with a knowing smirk. "Masie."

She rubbed the back of her neck. "Kerr," she replied.

The stable lad brought out two horses. Masie welcomed

the distraction. "I thought all three of us were going," Masie said.

"Aye," Bhaltair answered. "Ye ride wit' one of us."

"Ye dinnae trust me no' to flee, do ye?" Masie asked Bhaltair.

"I'm taking precautions, 'tis all."

"Brother, that's the wisest thing ye've said all day." Kerr checked his saddle.

It hadn't gone unnoticed, the grin the brothers shared. Both were strikingly handsome in their own way. Both had dark hair. Bhaltair's was curly while Kerr's was longer, shoulder-length. Bhaltair was gentle with boyish charm. Kerr was every bit a vigorous warrior. She bet if Kerr smiled more often, the brothers shared the same dimpled cheeks. However, out of the two, there was only one who made her heart quicken. But he saw her as the enemy.

Not wanting to be close to Kerr unnecessarily, Masie walked over to Bhaltair. "I'll ride with ye."

Bhaltair smiled. "I was hoping ye'd say that." He picked her up and placed her on the horse, then quickly mounted.

Kerr rode ahead.

It was another overcast day, which Masie was thankful for. When Bhaltair had invited her out, he wasn't taking no for an answer. She only prayed the sun would stay hidden and he kept his hands to himself.

The wind blew and Masie shivered, cuddling deeper into her cloak.

"Ye cold, lass?" Bhaltair asked.

"A wee bit, but I'll be fine."

He removed his cloak and draped it over Masie's shoulders. Bhaltair pulled her closer and whispered in her ear. "Better?"

Masie swallowed, uncomfortable against his touch. "Aye,"

"Masie, I apologize for my behavior last night. It was wrong of me to kiss ye. I hope ye'll forgive me."

"Aye. Some people react to herbs differently than others. I'm just happy that ye are well."

"Thank ye for understanding. Though if I may be completely honest, I dinnae regret it."

Her body stiffened. Mayhap, she should have ridden with Kerr. Apparently, Bhaltair was still experiencing the side effects of her blood.

They reached the village and Bhaltair dismounted, then helped Masie down. Kerr tied the horses to a nearby tree. She looked around. Merchants were set up in two long rows of shops and tents, selling goods and food.

"Shall we?" Bhaltair held his arm out for her.

Masie smiled, accepting.

The hairs bristled on the back of her neck as Kerr's arm brushed against hers as he walked next to her. No matter how hard she tried to calm her thundering heart, it was of no use. Being this close to him heightened her senses, leaving her a lustful mess. As they strolled down the path between the stalls, Masie felt safe flanked by the Highland warriors. It reminded her of how her sisters always sheltered her.

Bhaltair pointed to a small kirk with stone crosses in the courtyard. "Last summer, our village suffered an attack, killing a lot of our people and destroying most everything here. The kirk has finally been rebuilt."

"Och, the bloody bastards," Kerr spat. "Justice was served swift and harsh."

"The kirk is beautiful. Do ye know who was responsible for the attack?" Masie asked.

"A group of thieves. No one we recognized," Bhaltair explained.

"I'm so sorry," Masie said. "Innocents often suffer such attacks."

"Aye, we live in troubled times when supporting the wrong king can verra well get ye killed. Clan fighting against clan, brother killing brother. 'Tis the way of the Highlands," Kerr said.

"Aye, the Gunns and Keiths have been feuding for decades. Generation after generation fosters the same hatred. Sometimes I forget what we're fighting for," Bhaltair said gravely.

"Och, Brother, I will no' forget."

"Can I speak freely, Laird?" Masie asked.

"Aye."

"I admire ye passion for country and clan, but 'tis the responsibility of each generation to change their fate. Ye can stop the fighting."

"Ye make a good point." Bhaltair patted her hand. "Unfortunately, politics get in the way."

"No' when ye rule wit' an iron fist." Kerr shook his hand in the air. "There will always be fighting. A warrior is perceived by how he swings his sword in battle."

"But brawn does no' make a man. 'Tis what's in here that counts." Bhaltair pointed to his heart.

Kerr rolled his eyes.

As the brothers argued back and forth, she ignored them, taking in the scenery. Something sweet permeating the air caught her attention. Rosemary and honey? Aye, that was exactly what she was smelling. Masie walked ahead, following the scent to a little auld woman selling fragrant soaps. She picked up a bar of soap and sniffed it. "'Tis rosemary, aye?" Masie asked.

"Aye, with honey."

"'Tis heavenly."

"'Tis my husband's favorite." The auld woman winked. "He says I smell like the sweetest flower in Scotland."

Masie's cheeks heated.

"My blends are quite popular with the lasses. Here." The woman took a bar from underneath the table and gave it to Masie. "This one will bring a lad to his knees. White roses and honey."

Masie smelled it.

The auld woman leaned in. "'Tis also good for cramps."

Masie coughed, surprised at the woman's blunt nature. She tried to give the soap back but the woman refused. "Nay, my gift to ye. Any friend of the laird's is a friend of mine."

"Thank ye." There was something refreshing about the woman's kind nature. She looked deeper into the woman's eyes. Aye, there was something very familiar, but she couldn't put her finger on it.

"There ye are," Bhaltair called out, startling her. "I see ye found Ms. Graham's soaps. They are verra popular wit' the lasses," Bhaltair said.

"Aye. Ms. Graham is verra talented," Masie agreed.

Masie nodded to the woman before she followed Bhaltair back down the village path.

"Seize the witch!" a voice rang out.

Instantly, Masie trembled as she quickly spun around expecting to find one of Cormag's men coming after her. To her relief, a throng raced to a wooden platform where five people were performing.

"The play is starting. Are ye coming, Kerr?"

"Ye should warn her." Kerr arched a brow.

Masie looked at the brothers. "Warn me about what?"

Before Masie knew what was happing, Bhaltair excitedly pulled her toward the stage. With her heart racing with excitement, she followed Bhaltair as he shouldered his way through the crowd, finding a spot in front of the stage.

Bhaltair leaned toward Masie. "These actors have performed in front of the king."

Relief washed over her. Thank the gods she wasn't witnessing an actual witch being hung, drawn, and quartered. Yet, the visual before her frightened her more.

A huge wooden dragon head sat on the forefront of the stage. His mouth was wide open and flames burned inside. Twin black horns stuck out from its head and his eyes glowed red. Indeed, a fierce beastie. The actors were dancing provocatively in front of the dragon as if they were conjuring demons.

Masie couldn't tear her eyes away from the madness unfolding before her, until she saw a black-cloaked woman in the middle of it all. Her arms were outstretched to the sky, her black hair flowed down to her waist. Her face was painted white and her lips were red. She opened her mouth and showed her fangs. Masie gasped, and her hand flew to her mouth. Masie couldn't believe what she was seeing and began to tremble.

All of sudden, men dressed in leather tunics with devil masks on came running out of the dragon's mouth with torches in their hands. They charged the dancers, herding them toward the open jaws of the dragon head, until they were engulfed in flames.

"Into the mouth of hell, sinners," the crowd chanted.

Masie franticly searched the faces in the audience. Fists pumped angrily in the air. They roared louder as two guards grabbed the fanged woman and lifted her over their shoulders. Kicking and screeching, they entered the mouth to hell.

Masie grabbed Kerr's hand tightly and looked away. The chanting became deafening and Masie couldn't stand it anymore. She buried her head in Kerr's chest, fear overtaking her. When was the play going to end?

KERR'S BREATH seized in his lungs as soon as Masie grabbed his hand. He didn't know what to do. Damn Bhaltair for not warning Masie about the violent play. She was clearly frightened.

Apprehensively, he placed his hand on her head. "Shh," he whispered, then did something surprising. He kissed the top of her head.

Masie looked up at him, their gazes locked. "Let's get ye out of here."

Masie nodded. "I can no' see any more of t-this madness."

He caressed her cheek. "Can ye make it back to the horses?"

"Aye."

Kerr smiled. "Follow me."

Holding her hand, Kerr lead her away from the stage and angry people.

"Stop," Masie called out breathlessly.

Kerr turned around. "Are ye well?"

"Nay." Masie bent over, resting her hands on her thighs. "I can no' catch my breath. I feel like I'm going to be sick."

God's bones, he didn't think he could stomach seeing Masie sick. He started pacing.

"Please," Masie begged. "Please stop. 'Tis no' helping my stomach."

Bhaltair finally caught up to them. "Why did ye leave?" he asked, looking at his brother.

"Ye fool." Kerr strode in front of Bhaltair. "Ye should have warned her how vulgar the play was. She's frightened to death."

Bhaltair glanced at Masie. "I'm sorry, lass. I—"

"What?" Masie exclaimed. "That I'd enjoy seeing such ruthlessness, such...such crudeness."

"Nay, I wanted ye to experience—"

"Hell!" Masie yelled.

"Let's get ye back to the castle." Kerr helped Masie to walk. "Once ye rest, ye'll feel much better."

Kerr picked Masie up and set her on his horse, then mounted behind her. Once again, he felt his body come alive as she snuggled against his chest, sweet and soft like a wee lamb. Strong, yet so delicate. He couldn't help but protect her.

The stable lad met Kerr outside the stable and took his horse as he carried Masie to the castle and up to her bedchamber. He laid her down on the bed, removed her shoes, and tucked her in underneath the warm furs. Once she was comfortable, he walked to the hearth and placed some peat on the flames.

Before he left, he walked back to the bed and watched Masie sleep. Her dark eyelashes rested on her creamy cheeks. Her lips were made for kissing. Before long, he vowed, he would kiss that luscious mouth. Her chest rose in a soothing rhythm. At least she was resting and far away from those horrific images.

God's teeth, he hoped his gut was wrong about her, she couldn't be a spy.

The memory of the fanged woman being thrown into the flames at the play had plagued Masie's dreams. She couldn't shake the bad feeling. Her gaze darted around the bedchamber as she sat up. Shadows swayed on the stone walls. The dogs outside barked and howled as if they were chasing something down. Mayhap the men from the play were coming to get her, to burn her just like the fanged woman. *Baobhan sith, like me and my sisters.* It was only a matter of time before they found out who she was. She didn't want to be around when the witch hunters came.

Masie padded over to the wash basin and splashed water on her face, scrubbing the nightmare from her eyes. She patted her skin dry with a square of linen. Still shaken from her dream, she looked under the bed and searched the dark corners. *Maiden, Mother, Crone. 'Tis only a dream.* Masie exhaled, frustrated for allowing herself to be easily frightened. But the fear was real.

Even as powerful as she was, she couldn't outrun or destroy an angry mob.

She had to find something to occupy her mind, to forget about those horrid images. She opened the trunk at the end of her bed and pulled out a green dress with matching slippers. Bhaltair had kept his word and made sure she had clean clothes to wear. The trunk was filled with dresses, shifts, and shoes, more than she needed.

The dress fit perfectly, snug around her breasts and

tapered into a full skirt. Her mother's brooch sat on the table next to the bed. She pinned it on the inside of her dress, next to her heart.

The cold air would do her good, so Masie left the bedchamber and rushed downstairs and out the door. She didn't know where she was headed, and cared little as long as she wasn't stuck inside that nightmare.

She took the cobblestone path down into the bailey. It wasn't long until she found herself standing in the stable, stroking her horse's mane. Her soul was lost. She didn't have a home or a clan to call her own. Where did she fit in?

She liked Wickshire. But if the townsfolk found out what she was, they'd kill her.

It was ridiculous to desire the unattainable. A home, family, and most of all, a man who could love her—*all* of her. Every time Kerr was close by, he brought out those feelings. She couldn't explain it, she just wanted to be near him, wanted to know what made him happy. She wanted to know everything about him.

Masie, ye're the enemy. His words were unforgettable.

Time here was coming to end. It was rather silly to think she'd be welcomed into the mortal world. She could still hear the queen's warning, once a mortal finds the unexplainable a threat, they destroy it out of fear.

"Planning yer escape?" Kerr's voice slithered up her spine. Goddess, why did he have this effect on her? Her body tingled and he hadn't even touched her.

She whipped around. "Are ye following me?

"Nay, I have men that will do that for me." He winked and walked to his horse.

He still didn't trust her. *Masie, ye're the enemy.* "I know, I know," she whispered, trying to stop her nagging conscious.

"Did ye say something?" Kerr looked at her, brows furrowed.

"Nay—I mean—Are ye going for a ride?" Goddess, she was at a loss for words.

"Aye." He studied her for a moment. "Would ye like to join me?"

"Ye trust me no' to run?"

"Aye, yer sisters are still here. Ye wouldn't leave them."

He was right, she wouldn't. Her stomach fluttered thinking about being alone with him.

"I promise to be a proper gentleman."

Please, dinnae.

Kerr returned to saddling his horse. "I just thought ye might want a change of scenery. I'm sorry if I crossed the line."

That line had already been breached. He'd seen her naked.

"Aye, I'll join ye. Can I ride my horse? I've missed her dearly."

Again, she'd fallen under his suspicious eye. "What's the harm if ye know I will no' escape?"

"Och, lass, I trust ye. Ye can ride yer horse."

She let out an excited squeal.

"But..." He stepped in front of her. "Do no' mistake my kindness as weakness."

The intensity he displayed rendered her speechless. "Kerr, I'd never take yer kindness for granted, nor would I think ye as weak."

"Good." He walked back to his horse and mounted. "Now, keep up."

Before Masie could think, she mounted and raced out of the stable. She didn't need a saddle to ride. Leaning over her horse, Masie whispered, "Fly." Without delay, her mare galloped like hell through the bailey, easily catching up with Kerr.

They raced each other deep into the glen, weaving between trees. Masie took a measurable lead when the forest opened into a clearing. She slowed her horse and encouraged the beast to walk around in a circle to catch her breath. That's when she heard something from beyond the trees. She smiled. "Come out ye coward. There's no shame in being bested by a lass." No reply came. *He couldn't be that far behind, could he?* Was he hurt? She began to panic. "Kerr, 'tis no' funny." She searched the tree line for movement.

Happiness quickly turned to panic and she jumped down, feeling shaky. Sweat beaded on her forehead. Goddess, she couldn't breathe. She fell to her knees, sucking in air.

"Masie!" Kerr came running from the opposite side of the glen. "What is it?" He cradled her in his arms. "Masie, talk to me."

As soon as she saw his face, she calmed down. "Dinnae ever do that to me again."

"Do what? Best ye?"

"I was here first."

"Are ye sure, because I was right over there setting up a target when I saw ye reach the clearing." He pointed.

Masie stood, shaking away the nerves. "Ye should have answered me. I dinnae see ye over there."

"I wanted to surprise ye." Kerr lead her to the target. "Have ye ever shot a bow?"

"Nay."

"I thought ye should learn how. I saw how upset and frightened ye were yesterday and I want to teach ye so ye can protect yerself."

Masie regarded his words. He wanted to teach her how

to defend herself? She didn't know how to take his sudden kindness. Yesterday, he took her away from that violent play and now he wanted to teach her how to shoot a bow. Why the sudden change of heart? "Are ye sure ye can trust the enemy with an arrow?"

Kerr smirked. "Aye, 'tis my heart I dinnae know about."

Kerr pulled an arrow from a quiver leaning against a tree. He stood a distance away from the target and readied the bow. "Watch carefully." He drew back, then let go. The arrow landed in the center of the target. He grabbed another arrow. "Come." He motioned for her to stand in front of him. "Yer stance is verra important. Feet should be shoulder width apart." He gripped her hips, moving her into position. "And stand up straight."

Taking in a shaky breath, she inhaled his scent as he wrapped his arms around her, positioning the bow. He slid her hair to the side, her neck exposed to his lips. "Draw back." How was she supposed to pay attention when he was awakening her desires? Goddess help her. "Now, let go." His lips brushed against her ear softly and her insides melted. Aye, she wanted to let go and kiss him, but that's not what he meant. She leaned into him, giving him a sideways glance. "Ye're distracting me."

He grinned and took a step back. Masie aimed and the arrow sailed through the air, splintering the center of the target. "Ha, did ye see that!" Excitedly, she turned to Kerr. "I hit it!"

"Ye're a natural. It takes most people several shots before they even hit the target."

"And I've bested ye." She gave him a playful shove.

"Och," he grumbled. "I was warming up. Another round?"

"Aye." She tipped her chin up, accepting the challenge.

9

THE NEXT MORN, Masie raced to her sisters' chamber. She knocked on the door. After spending a day with Kerr and sharing an evening meal together, she was going to burst if she didn't tell someone about it. When no one answered, she opened the door. "Adaira? Leana?"

Since they didn't have kitchen duty, she thought they might be in the great hall. Quickly, Masie went downstairs. Adaira sat in front of a loom weaving and Leana was next to her working on needlepoint.

"Taking a liking to weaving?" Masie asked.

"Aye, 'tis a good way to listen to gossip around the castle." Adaira smiled. "See that man over there?" She gestured toward him.

Masie looked over shoulder. "Aye."

"His been having an affair with one of the kitchen servants."

"How do ye know?"

"Watch."

A lass walked over to the man. She leaned into him, her breasts exposed from the top of her dress as she poured him ale. The man winked and nodded toward the kitchen. The lass filled two more tankards, then sauntered away.

Masie gave Adaira a sideways glare. "Adaira, that does no' mean he's having an affair. All he did was smile at the lass."

"Nay, keep watching."

Masie huffed and rolled her eyes, irritated at her sister's behavior. She watched the man finish his ale, wipe his mouth with the back of his hand, and then nonchalantly follow the lass to the kitchen.

"See, 'tis good to be aware of yer surroundings." Adaira winked.

Masie giggled. "Nay, 'tis gossip."

Even Leana laughed. Masie smiled at her. "It makes me happy to see ye smile again."

Leana turned her attention back to her needlepoint.

"My shoulders are stiff, Masie. Would ye mind helping me weave?" Adaira asked.

"Aye." She took her sister's seat as Adaira stood and stretched.

"I think I might have found a way to escape," Adaira said.

Masie's eyes grew wide and a lump formed in her chest with the thought of leaving. "How?"

Adaira sat down next to Leana. "The other night I was sitting at the window in our bedchamber and I saw a ladder right outside the window leading to the battlements. I haven't climbed out there, but it looks promising."

Masie weaved a strand of wool. "It sounds too dangerous."

"Aye," Adaira agreed. "But with the castle heavily guarded, I dinnae see another option."

Her sister was right. Masie had tried an easier way and

failed or was she rationalizing with herself, searching for an excuse not to go?

"Sister." Adaira eyed Masie suspiciously. "Do ye fancy the laird?"

"Nay." Masie shook her head.

"Ye can no' lie to me. I can feel it."

"Even if I did, I wouldn't tell ye. And 'tis no' the laird I fancy."

"His brother?"

Masie kept silent, her beaming smile giving her away.

"Ye be playing with fire. Mortals dinnae understand our kind."

"Dinnae ye think I know," Masie bit back. "Besides, we're the enemy."

"Guard yer heart, sweet lass," Adaira said. "Heartache is far worse than any pain ye'll ever endure."

Masie stopped working. There was something hidden behind her sister's words. "Can I ask ye a question?"

"Aye."

"Have ye ever been heartbroken?"

Adaira looked away. She exhaled. "Aye, and I've been the one who broke a heart. I beg ye to think twice before giving yer heart away."

It was just like Adaira to protect her from danger. She was always the voice of reason and possessed an unwavering strength Masie admired.

"I will." Masie hugged her sister. "Besides, the three of us are stuck together. There's no room for a fourth."

Adaira smiled at her.

"Who's that?" Adaira asked as she pointed behind her.

Masie turned around. "Rabbie. Are ye looking for yer uncle?'

"Nay." The lad eyed the loom.

"Do ye weave?"

"Nay. Uncle Kerr says a lad should spend his time wielding a sword."

"Och, how do ye think the tales of battles and warriors live on?"

The lad looked at her, his brows creased.

"Rabbie, the tapestries hanging throughout the castle display stories of famous battles and the men who fought for what they believe in. Without it, how would their tales be known?"

"Can ye teach me how to weave a story?"

Masie didn't know what to say. Children were as foreign to her as a man's touch. "Aye." Masie smiled.

The lad's face beamed with delight.

"Here." Masie scooted over. "Come sit and I'll show ye."

Kerr entered the great hall after a full day of hunting deer. Successful, he'd downed two bucks and a boar. Though he tried to forget the way Masie made him feel, it was impossible to keep fighting against it. Over the last two days, she'd consumed him. She had him by the ballocks, thinking about a future. A wife—children. God's bones, the lass twisted his thoughts. He was a warrior. The call of battle forever in his blood. No woman was going to change his heart.

Exhausted and hungry, Kerr set off to the kitchen, pushing Masie far away from his thoughts.

"Kerr!" A lass strode across the hall.

His patience had already been tested. He was in no mood to hear Ina's problems or to ward off her bold advances. The woman was trouble. He proceeded to seek out ale. Thankful he didn't have to go far, a lass poured him a tankard. He didn't quite make it across the room before Ina cornered him.

"May I have a word with ye?" she asked.

"Nay," Kerr said dryly. "I'm tired and need sleep." He stepped aside, but Ina blocked him.

"'Tis about the Keith girls. The blonde one."

Kerr took a long pull of ale. He slammed the empty tankard on the table, then crossed his arms across his chest. God's bones, he couldn't escape Masie.

Ina smiled in victory. "'Tis no' safe to allow her to walk freely among the clan."

"And why is that?"

"She's no' like us, Kerr. I can no' put my finger on it, but there's something different about her."

"Ina, I think ye daft."

"Ye're defending a Keith. The enemy."

Before he said something he'd regret later, he clenched his jaw tight.

Ina placed her hands on her hips. "Och, while ye were out hunting, Rabbie spent the day with the wench."

"Rabbie?"

"Aye. And I'm sure she's cast her wickedness on him. Yer sister would no' approve of such behavior."

Kerr grabbed Ina's arms and pinned her with a glare. "Ye will no' speak of Glenna in that tone. And Rabbie is no concern of yers."

Ina held his gaze. "Then ye better do right by Rabbie, for that matter, the clan. Be rid of the Keith wenches or I'll get rid of them meself."

Kerr reeled in his anger and released Ina. "Are ye questioning my ability to care for my nephew?"

"Nay, I—"

"Trust me, Ina, if ye cause any trouble with the Keith girls, I will personally see ye hung for treason."

"Treason?"

"Aye, they are the laird's guests. No harm will be brought upon them." Kerr leaned in close and whispered in her ear, "If ye want to keep yer pretty head, I warn ye to keep to yer own affairs." Kerr pushed past her and made his way through the great hall.

He took in a deep breath, calming himself. He needed to find Rabbie and see he was well. He didn't search for long. In a corner of the hall his nephew was sitting with Masie...weaving?

Kerr approached the two. He stood with his arms crossed over his chest.

"Uncle!" Rabbie jumped from his seat and hugged him. "Miss Masie and I have been weaving all day."

Masie stood and smiled. "He's a verra smart lad. A quick learner."

Kerr looked down at Rabbie. "And do ye feel this was time well spent, sewing all day?"

The lad adverted his gaze. "Nay."

"A lad should be practicing with a sword, no' playing with string."

"Kerr," Masie interrupted. "'Tis my fault. I lost track of the day. Dinnae blame Rabbie."

He pinned Masie with a hard glare. "Rabbie, go to bed. I'll be up to tuck ye in."

"Aye, Uncle." He turned to Masie. "Thank ye."

Masie nodded. After the child was gone, she made her way to the stairs. "Kerr Gunn, ye are something else."

Kerr followed right behind her. He was something else? Nay. She had no right to scold him. Aye, he was harsh on the lad, but he'd never seen Rabbie take to a lass besides his sister. It had shaken him to see Masie in that role.

"I'm no' a fool. I can see what ye're doing."

"And what might that be?"

"I saw ye kissing Bhaltair."

Masie shook her head and continued up the stairs.

They reached the landing. "Dinnae walk away from me. I want to know the truth. I'm tired of ye playing wit' my mind," Kerr said.

Masie whipped around. "Just what are ye saying?"

"Dinna play sweet and innocent wit' me. Ye pretended to be the lass in distress yesterday so ye could play on my emotions. I saw ye kissing Bhaltair. Ye want something lass and I will no' be the fool to fall for yer games."

"Och, I understand. This is about yer crushed ego." Masie jabbed a finger at his chest. "First, Bhaltair kissed me. Secondly, I have had enough of yer suspicions. For the last time, I'm no' a spy. I obey yer rules, I've saved yer brother from sure death, and have only showed kindness to yer people. What is it about me that repulses ye so?" Her blue eyes bore straight through him.

He grabbed her by the waist and pulled her against him, his body blazing as her breasts pressed against his chest. Glaring into her eyes, an animalistic urge surfaced, driving him to claim her right there. "Every time ye touch or look at Bhaltair, I'm blinded by rage. I want ye hands on me, Masie, and only me."

He snaked his hand behind her neck, pulling her closer. Inside, reasoning battled with his urge to surrender to the power she held over him. He belonged on the battlefield not in a lass's arms. "Lass, ye dinnae repulse me. Ye have bewitched me." He claimed her lips, kissing her deeply.

He expected a smack but didn't get one. She parted her

lips and allowed him a taste. A sweetness washed over his tongue like warm honey. Her body was soft and fit against him perfectly. He knew one taste would be his undoing.

"Masie," he whispered, brushing his lips against hers. "I'm an arse. Please, forgive me."

"Aye, ye are an arse." She grinned up at him. "'Tis no' yer brother that makes my heart skip beats. 'Tis ye." She stepped out from his embrace and continued down the corridor.

Damn the devil! How could she say such things and walk away? He watched her until she disappeared around the corner. The desire to run after the lass consumed him, yet he couldn't do it. He thought about throwing her over his shoulder and taking her to his bedchamber, making love to her until the morn. But he needed to make things right with Rabbie first, then he'd find his blue-eyed lass.

10

MASIE TOUCHED her kiss-swollen lips and grinned. Kerr Gunn desired her. Her heart still fluttered and her knees threatened to buckle. No man had never made her feel like this. He was pure, raw male, mysterious, dominate, but most of all, he took her breath away. He'd captured her heart.

She'd been deep into her musings and hadn't realized she'd passed her bedchamber. She thought to turn around and make her way back, but a nearby door that stood ajar caught her attention. She opened it all the way. "Hello?"

No one replied, so she walked in.

A desk and chair sat in front of the hearth. A map of Caithness was laid out. "Och." Just what she needed.

Masie studied the area on the map just north of the village of Wickshire, where a small drawing of a castle marked the page. Coastline dominated the east side of Wick. The castle was flanked by cliffs. The only way out was south, which wasn't an option. Dornoch occupied the south. "'Tis a challenge, indeed," she huffed. There had to be a different way out.

Looking up from the map, Masie spied a tapestry

hanging next to a book shelf. She walked over to it, taking in the scene. She traced the black raven crest on the Highlander's armor. He was fighting his way through a throng of Keith men. As Masie took in more, she saw who the man was fighting for—a beautiful woman with flowing red hair. She was with a man from Clan Keith on horseback, crying and reaching for the warrior from Clan Gunn.

Along the border of the tapestry, ravens circled a herd of fleeing stags. "Clan Gunn and Clan Keith," Masie said, astounded by the detailed embroidery.

"That's my father. The honorable Alex Gunn, Laird of Caithness, Earl of Wickshire."

Masie whipped around to find Kerr standing in the doorway. "'Tis a stunning piece," she said.

"Aye." Kerr walked into the solar, the grim lines on his face noticeable.

"Who is the woman? Is she yer mum?"

"Nay." Kerr poured two drams of whiskey and handed one to Masie. He stood next to her, looking at the tapestry. "I dinnae know her, yet I've lived with her ghost all of my life."

Masie wanted to know more, but she didn't want to meddle in his affairs. "She's verra beautiful."

"The story my father told me growing up was the woman in the tapestry was taken from him on their wedding day by a Clan Keith warrior. He fought for years to get her back, but Laird Doughall hid her away. Finally, Father gave up. He loved her until his last breath."

"What about yer mum?"

"Och, she never had a chance against the woman's ghost. My father married her out of duty not love."

Moments passed in silence as they looked at the tapestry together. Masie took his hand in hers. "I'm terribly sorry for yer loss."

"Och." He kissed the back of her hand. "Helen's ghost died with him."

Masie's heart dove straight into her stomach. Her mother's name was Helen. She looked closer at the red-headed figure. *Mum?*

"Come sit wit' me." Kerr brought her over to a bench and they sat down. "All my life I've fought for my clan, fought for justice. I dinnae have room in my heart for anything else."

Masie stared at a cracked stone on the wall, trying not to cry. *'Tis for the best.*

"Yet, somehow, ye've breached the walls. 'Tis no' like me to fall for a lass as easily as I've fallen for ye."

Masie's palms were sweaty and her heart raced again.

"I need the truth, lass. Who ye are and why were ye on the battlefield."

His smoldering eyes were full of passion. She was stuck between two unhappy choices. There was nothing more she wanted than to be honest with him, yet she couldn't open her heart.

"Kerr, I'm no' like other lasses."

"Dinnae ye think I know that? The moment I laid eyes on ye I knew it."

"Nay, ye took me prisoner," she teased.

"Because I couldn't let ye go." Kerr placed his hand on the back of her neck and pulled her close until their foreheads touched. "Masie," he whispered against her lips before he kissed her.

His kiss seared her cold flesh and she wanted more. She opened her mouth, breathing him in. As he slowly slid his tongue between her lips, a shockwave rippled to her core. The taste of whiskey played on her tongue and made her stomach flutter. She threaded her fingers through his hair, drawing him in deeper.

Kerr broke the kiss, then cupped her face. She didn't want the kiss to end. "I need to know."

Masie looked up into his eyes. "I can't. If ye know what's best, ye'll let me go and never look back."

Kerr's hands slipped from her face. The sorrow she saw in his eyes shook her soul.

"I can no' permit it," he said.

"Please, forgive me, Kerr. I wish my life wasn't so complicated." She forced herself to her feet, for if she stayed any longer, she'd give in, telling him everything. That's what her heart wanted, but her voice of reason told her differently. Without looking back at him, she left the solar, tears burning her eyes.

11

MASIE RACED TO HER SISTERS' bedchamber, crying. She couldn't breathe, her chest ached. What was it about him that captivated her? Why Kerr? Why a mortal? Masie swiped at a tear trickling down her cheek. She wished they never stopped to feed on the battlefield. She wished her fate hadn't been changed.

Not watching where she was going, Masie rounded the corner and slammed into a woman. Her blood boiled when she realized who it was. The brunette from the great hall.

"Witch," the woman spat, hate burning in her eyes.

Masie unleashed her fury, pushing her against the wall. She grabbed a fistful of the woman's dress and hissed through fanged teeth.

Terror-stricken, the woman gasped. "I knew it! Ye're a monster."

A monster? Aye. The demon inside released, her vision burned red, and normal movements raced by her with super speed. An image flashed in her mind, she was ripping the wench's throat out, making her feel every last drop of pain while she fed from her.

"And I haven't eaten in days," Masie growled.

The woman grabbed her neck, hiding it from Masie.

"Masie!"

Slowly, she turned her head, vaguely recognizing the voice.

"Walk away." Adaira approached cautiously. "Ye dinnae want to do something daft."

Masie let go and took a step back as the woman ran for her life down the corridor.

"Masie, have ye gone mad?"

"I-I"

"Ye weren't thinking. Ye need to control yer temper."

"Aye." Once Masie fully understood the ramifications of her actions, she looked at her sister, shocked at what she'd just done. "I'm so sorry. I dinnae know what came over me."

Adaira wrapped her arm around Masie's shoulders as they walked back to their bedchamber. By the morn, the witch hunters would be kicking down her door. They had to leave tonight.

Masie stopped. "We must go."

"How? Do ye have a plan? Because every nook and crevice in the castle is heavily guarded."

"Aye, but if we dinnae leave, I'm afraid by morn the witch hunters will come. I saw a map in the solar. If we head west, we'll have a chance. Clan Gunn's land has a wide reach and we can no' go south."

"Aye," Adaira agreed. "I might be able to help."

Masie followed Adaira into the bedchamber. "We'll need our horses. We can no outrun the guards on foot. There's too many of them."

"The trick will be making it to the stable without getting caught."

Adaira ripped the furs from the window.

"What are ye doing?" Masie asked as she donned her cloak.

"Escaping."

"From the window?" Masie thought it the daftest idea she'd heard. "We'll fall to our death. I dinnae think Leana is well enough to travel, let alone climb a ladder up a castle wall."

"Sister, I'll be fine." The sound of Leana's voice made Masie's breath hitch.

"Leana." She rushed to her sister, hugging her. "I've been so worried about ye. Ye haven't said a word since—" Masie paused, not wanting old memories to surface and cause Leana to slip back into shock.

"Oh, my sweet Masie." Leana tightened her arms around her. It was just then Masie knew she had her sister back. "I'm ready to leave this place."

Adaira put her hands on her hips. "How do ye expect us to escape? By walking out the front door?"

"Do ye have a better idea?" Masie spouted.

"Remember the ladder I told ye about?" Adaira asked.

"Aye."

"The only other way out of the castle is through the battlements. The other night I climbed the ladder and found what I think is a secret passage out."

Masie had a difficult time trusting Adaira's plan, but she knew she was right. She'd lost control of her anger and jeopardized their safety. She'd accept her sister's plan.

Masie walked over to the window, observing the thin ledge. *Maiden, mother, crone.* "If ye think 'tis best, then I'll do it." "Masie, whatever happens, promise me ye'll never look back. Keeping running."

She shook her head, for she couldn't swallow past the nervous lump in her throat.

Adaira leapt up on the window ledge, then faced Masie. "And dinnae look down." She winked.

Masie rolled her eyes. When she couldn't see Adaira anymore, Masie followed her sister's lead. Before she took the first step off the window ledge, she glanced at Leana. Her sister smiled, encouraging her. Masie looked up and climbed on the ladder, following Adaira up the wall.

The wind blew, her cloak snapping in the air. Masie fought the urge to look down. Aye, she was immortal and the fall wouldn't kill her, but she'd feel every broken bone in her body. She'd never experienced anything of that nature and wasn't going to start tonight.

Adaira finally reached the battlements. Masie caught up with her. One more step and she could reach her sister's hand.

"Make haste, Masie," Adaira called out.

She climbed the last step and reached up, barely brushing the tips of Adaira's fingers. "I can no' reach."

"Keep trying, Masie." Adaira encouraged. "We dinnae have time to waste."

As she tried again, her foot slipped and she lost her grip. Chunks of rock crumbled from the wall as she held on with one hand. Terrified, her body swayed, her feet dangling. Masie peered down—she was going to die.

"Masie, grab my hand!"

With all her might, Masie swung her body back against the wall and desperately tried to reach her sister's hand, praying she wouldn't end up falling. In one swift motion, Masie felt herself being pulled up and over the battlement wall.

"Masie, dinnae ever scare me like that again." Adaira hugged her sister.

"Dinnae fash yerself. I'll never climb a castle wall again."

"Dinnae worry," Leana called out sarcastically as she heaved herself up and over the wall. "I dinnae need any help."

Once all three girls were safely on the battlements, Adaira led them to a door. She opened it, revealing a narrow stairwell that twisted down into the darkness. "Masie, ye go first."

Masie's eyes widened. "Why?"

"Ye would rather stay here and burn?" Adaira bit back.

Masie shook her head. Adaira pushed her forward. Every step she took felt like she was descending into a black pit. Usually, she'd be able to see in the dark, but her nerves were besting her. If they were caught...she shook the thought free.

She swatted at cobwebs, held her breath through the dank smell of death, and jumped once or twice from something furry running across her foot. The stairs finally came to end. A wood door blocked their exit from the stairwell. Masie pushed and pushed, but the door wouldn't budge. "The door is stuck."

"It must open," Adaira said as she pushed on the door with Massie.

With all their might, the three sisters forced it open. They tumbled through it, landing on the ground. Masie gasped, her eyes widened as she saw where they were. Waves crashed into the cliffs, spraying sea water into the air. One more step forward and she would be swimming with the fish.

She retreated from the edge. "That was close."

"We need to keep moving." Adaira grabbed Masie's arm, helping her up.

"Aye," Masie agreed. "From what I can recall from the map, we're on the east side of the castle."

"Good. Keep to the shadows and follow me," Adaira instructed.

With their backs flat against the castle wall, they made it unseen to the stables. The next challenge, getting by the guards.

Masie heard footsteps and men talking. "Shite, guards!"

Adaira pressed her finger to her lips. "Shh." She held her arm against Masie's chest, pushing her back as two guards passed by.

Masie's heart was beating so fast she didn't know how much more she could take.

"See the cart next to the tree?" Adair whispered.

Masie searched the area. "Aye."

"If we hide there, we'll be closer to the stables, but we'll have to make a run for it."

Masie nodded.

"Remember what I said?" Adaira asked.

"Dinnae look back. Keep moving."

"Good. Now run."

Masie hiked up her dress and took off in a full run. Her legs pumped faster and faster.

"Halt!" a guard shouted out.

Shite!

Masie looked back. The guard was following her. *Keep running!*

"Masie, go!" Adaira called out, gaining the attention of the guard.

As Masie looked back, horror ripped through her. The guard was now running after Adaira and Leana, heading in the opposite direction of the cart. *Nay!* Masie halted. They can no' leave me. She began to run after them.

Someone grabbed her arm, keeping her from moving. "Come, child."

Masie yanked free and when she looked up, saw it was the auld woman from the village. "I have to save them."

"Nay, lass. Ye need to get to safety."

"I must go after them." The woman grabbed her around the waist, stopping her. "Yer sisters wanted ye safe. Why do ye think they drew the guard's attention? Ye will no' spoil their bravery."

"Please, I have to go." Masie fought the woman's hold, but the sheer thought of her sisters in danger made her weak. "Adaira! Leana!" She screamed and reached out to them as the woman dragged her to the cart.

She lost sight of her sisters and she fell to the ground sobbing. What was she going to do without Adaira and Leana? What if they were fleeing right into the grasp of Cormag? Flooded by despair, she knew there was nothing she could do to help them.

"Hurry child, we must go." The woman helped her up and Masie followed her to the cart.

She climbed into the back of the wooden cart and sat on top of a pile of hay. She just hoped it wasn't full of cow dung.

"Stay put or yer sisters' effort will be for naught. Promise me ye will no' try to escape."

Too exhausted to move, Masie nodded.

"Good. Relax, child, everything will be well." The woman gave her a smile.

Minutes later, the cart was rolling forward and she heard the woman click her tongue at her horse. She lay back in the hay, tears streaming down her face. "Why Adaira, why did ye leave me?" she sobbed. Would she ever see her again?

Masie curled into a ball, tugging her cloak around her cold body. She reached into the top of her dress and pulled out her mother's brooch. She kissed the only thing she had left of her family, then squeezed the metal in her hand. "Maiden, mother, crone, please watch over Adaira and Leana." She repeated her prayer over and over again until she fell asleep.

12

BHALTAIR SAT in his chair behind his table with a heavy heart, holding a missive. He'd broken the seal moments ago and still couldn't believe what he'd read. He leaned back and sighed. What was he going to do? Frankly, it was too early in the morn to be making such decisions. He scratched his chin and reread the missive, hoping by chance he'd missed something.

"Nay." Bhaltair exhaled. "Murder?"

A knock at the door interrupted his thought.

Kerr entered the room. "Ye wanted to see me, Brother?"

"Aye, I'm afraid I've received some disturbing news." Bhaltair stood and walked over to Kerr, handing him the missive.

Giving his brother a concerned look, Kerr took the missive.

Bhaltair walked to the window, looking across the bailey, waiting for his brother's response.

"Shite. Murder?"

"Aye," Bhaltair said. "According to Laird Keith, Masie

and her sisters are wanted for questioning in the murder of his son. Does no' look good for the girls."

Kerr dropped the parchment on the desk. "What are ye going to do?"

"If we dinnae return the Keith girls willingly, they'll come and take them by force."

"Another war."

"Aye." Bhaltair exhaled.

Kerr shook his head." Something does no' feel right. Masie couldn't be capable of murder."

Surprised by his statement, Bhaltair glanced at his brother. "Ye've had a change of heart?"

"I can no' explain it. Masie's—"

"An angel."

"Aye."

"Ye dinnae have to tell me. I felt her magic, too. I couldn't be more proud than to have Masie Keith as part of our family."

Kerr swallowed. "Och, I'm no' talking about forever."

Bhaltair grinned. "I know. But I've seen how she looks at ye. If ye dinnae make an honest lass out of her, I will."

"So what are ye going to do?"

"I've sent Liam to fetch the girls. I want to hear their side of the story."

"And if Masie or one of her sisters murdered Laird Keith's son, what shall we do?"

Liam rushed into the solar. "My laird." He bowed.

"Aye?"

"The Keith girls are gone."

"What do ye mean, gone?" Kerr advanced on Liam and grabbed a handful of his tunic. "What did ye do?"

"Nothing. I swear on my father's grave. I was asked to fetch the girls and when I went to their bedchamber, they were gone. I had the rest of the men search the castle. 'Tis like they vanished."

Kerr let go of Liam's tunic. "Bhaltair, we must find Masie before Laird Keith does."

"Aye. Gather yer men. We'll ride out together."

With haste, Kerr left the solar with Liam. Bhaltair grabbed his sword and followed behind. For his brother's sake, they had to find Masie. There had to be an explanation. He just hoped she was innocent, for war was about to break out.

13

THE CART JOSTLED and jumped over uneven ground, waking Masie as she hit her head on a trunk. How long had she slept? Masie sat up, trying to figure out where the woman was traveling to. With speed, the cart wove through the trees as the auld woman raced her horses through the thick vegetation. Barely missing a low laying branch, Masie ducked and closed her eyes tight. *Maiden, Mother, Crone! The woman's trying to kill me.*

The horses slowed down and Masie drew in a breath of relief. She opened her eyes. They were in the middle of the glen, not a soul in sight.

"Whoa, beasties," the woman called out.

Pulling straw from her hair, Masie sat on her knees, ready to get out of the rickety cart. Her head pounded from being thrown around. Mentally, she vowed never to ride with the auld woman again.

"Welcome home."

Cautiously, Masie stepped out and followed the woman into a cottage. Once inside, the small space seemed quite cozy. A black pot hung over a fire pit in the middle of the room. Two chairs and a table were off to the side and a pallet arranged in the corner.

"Is this yer home?" Masie asked.

"Nay, 'tis yers."

Masie looked around. "I can no' stay here. I must find my sisters."

"Sit." The woman pointed at the chair.

Masie obeyed, watching the woman's every move. "Why did ye help me escape?"

"Because a mum always protects their children." The auld woman stood in front of her and removed her cloak. Her hunched body straightened, her wrinkled skin smoothed, and her hooded eyes changed to a vibrant blue. She shook her head and the white strands of her hair turned bright red.

"Mum?" Masie jumped out of her chair, knocking it over. "'Tis a dream. They all said ye were dead."

"Masie, my sweetling. The moment I saw ye in the village, I knew I had to tell ye the truth."

Masie threw her arms around her. "I'm so sorry, Mum," she sniffled. "We should have listened. The queen did verra bad things to us."

"Shh, my sweet. 'Tis I that should have been honest wit' ye."

Masie stepped out of her embrace. "What do ye mean?"

Helen picked up the chair and joined her daughter. "My sister is Queen Galanthus Snowdrop, the Winter Fae Queen and ruler of the Unseelies. Her heart is as twisted as the branches of a blackthorn. I'm afraid she took her vengeance out on my children.

Masie looked at her mother, puzzled.

"She wasn't always this evil. We were born into the Seelie fae court, living among the humans and playing in the sunlight. Until jealously clouded her heart when yer father took me as his bride instead of her. Soon after, she took her vows with the Unseelie to gain the power to one day take what she thought was rightfully hers, my children."

"Oh, Mum." Masie squeezed her hands.

"You girls were never meant to become *Baobhan sith*. A Seelie fae, aye. She tricked ye into taking a blood oath to the Unseelies."

Masie sat back, she couldn't believe what she was hearing. "Mum, we were only trying to save ye from Doughall, to change our fates. We wished upon a shooting star—"

"And she took yer innocence for granted. Trust me, Masie, my sister was waiting, lurking in the darkness to make her move."

"Then 'tis true. I am a monster."

"Sweetling, look at me." Her mother lifted her chin.

Goddess, she'd missed her mother's warmth.

"No one can change yer true heart. Ye're still my kindhearted, sweet wee lass." Helen caressed her cheek. "But all grown up now." She smiled. "A bonny lass, indeed."

Masie smiled. The last time she saw her mum, she was seven summers old. Dread filled her heart. They had escaped the queen only to find bigger trouble.

"Masie, what be on yer mind?"

"I dinnae know what to do. Leana is in trouble. I found her with two dead men on Samhain. One of them was Cormag's son."

Helen stood. "Did Leana kill him?"

"I want to believe she's innocent, but I saw the bite

marks on their necks. She does no' remember what happened." Masie exhaled. "There's more."

"More?" Helen moved to the window and looked out.

"We had to leave Dornoch. Cormag blamed us for his son's death. When we left, we were captured by Clan Gunn. They think we are spies for Clan Keith. Mum, I dinnae know what to do or who to trust." Masie swiped a tear from her cheek. "And now I'm alone."

Helen rushed over to Masie and hugged her. "Sweet lass. I was wondering how ye came across the Gunn lads."

Masie looked up at her. "I saw the tapestry in the lairds solar of ye. Is it true? Did Doughall take ye away from yer true love?'

Helen nodded. "Aye, but he gave me three of the most precious gifts. I can no' change the past. But I do know ye can trust Bhaltair and Kerr. They're like their father, good at heart."

Masie couldn't let go, she hugged her mother tightly. "I can no' believe ye're alive." Her mother ran her fingers through her hair, easing her worries. Oh, how she had missed her.

"Masie?"

"Aye?"

"Ye must promise me ye will no' tell anyone ye've seen me."

"Why? Aren't ye staying?"

"I wish I could. Trust in me, I'll see ye again verra soon."

With hesitation, Masie nodded. "I promise."

"Be careful, my sweet, the queen will soon come. This time we'll fight back."

Helen pulled on her cloak and walked to door.

"Mum," Masie called out and her mother turned.

"I love ye."

Her mother smiled. She blew Masie a kiss. "Verra soon."

The door shut. Masie sat on the pallet of furs staring at the door, hopeful her mother would return. She just had to come back, for she'd lost everything else already, her clan, sisters, and Kerr.

14

THE GUNN WARRIORS thundered through the glen, a pack of hunting dogs barking ahead. Kerr had to reach Masie before Cormag. God's bones, if the man laid a hand on her, he'd gut him. Anger beyond measure coursed through him. The lass would have been safe at Raven's Landing. He'd given his word that he'd protect her and her sisters. Why did she flee? Why didn't she trust him?

The dogs came to a stop. With their noses to the ground, they circled a small area. Kerr searched the forest for some sign, a broken tree branch, ripped clothing, anything giving him a clue.

He dismounted and examined the ground where the dogs were gathered. "Wheel tracks." He followed them off the path to a rocky trail. He whistled and the dogs came running, picking up the scent.

Kerr strode back to his horse and mounted.

"We'll find her, Brother." Bhaltair rode up next to Kerr.

"Aye. And when I do, I dinnae know if I should kiss her first or tan her hide." Kerr kicked his horse forward and followed the dogs.

"Och, I say both. But something is telling me she's no' the taming type. Reminds me of someone I know." Bhaltair grinned at Kerr.

Aye, Masie indeed wasn't a meek lass. Her stubborn streak set him ablaze. She was coming back with him to Wickshire even if he had to throw her over his shoulder kicking and screaming.

Hours later, night had fallen, making it hard to search the forest. He was tired, hungry, and needed to piss in the worst way. He halted his horse and raised his hand, signaling his men to stop. "We'll camp here tonight and resume our search in the early morn."

While his men hurried to make camp, Kerr sought out a place to relieve himself. He found a tree to stand behind and something caught his attention in the valley below. Through the moonlight he spied a cottage. Could Masie be inside? It would explain the hounds picking up her scent on the trail. His heart raced. Quickly, Kerr returned to his horse.

"Where are ye going?" Bhaltair asked.

"I saw a cottage. I'm going to search it."

"Nay, no' alone. Could be a trap. I'll go with ye."

"Brother, stay here with the men and rest. Eat. I'll be careful." Kerr rode off without further explanation.

"Ye stubborn, fool," Bhaltair called out.

As Kerr approached the cottage, he slowed his horse and dismounted. A horse was tied to a tree nearby which meant someone had to be inside. There was no smoke billowing from the roof. It was too cold outside to not have a fire. Kerr unsheathed his sword, ready to fight if he had to. His skin pricked, warning him to tread softly. It could be a trap as his brother suggested.

Kerr opened the door. If someone was here why wasn't it locked? He walked in. The room was dark, cold, and looked to be empty. He let his guard down, no one was about. The loss of hope swirled in his gut; he'd hoped to see Masie inside.

"Shite." He walked outside and searched the tree line. "Where are ye Masie?" he whispered into the night sky.

"I'm right here." He heard Masie's sweet voice from behind and turned around.

Her blue eyes stole his breath. Delicate, yet deadly to his heart. He took her in his arms and claimed her soft lips so passionately it shook his soul. She was safe.

He broke the kiss, leaving Masie breathless. "Why did ye leave me?"

"I had to."

"Masie, I know yer secret. We need to talk. But first I need to start a fire. 'Tis colder than a witch's heart out here."

"Aye." Masie followed Kerr inside where he started a fire in the pit. She lit a few candles, setting them throughout the room.

Kerr stood, looking into the flames, rubbing his cold hands together. "Masie, come sit. We need to talk."

Masie sat with her hands in her lap, nervously biting her bottom lip.

"There's no need to be anxious. I know why ye left Dornoch. Bhaltair received a missive from Cormag Keith stating he wants ye and yer sisters to be brought back for questioning about his son's murder. All I ask is ye tell me the truth."

"Are ye going to send me back?" Masie looked up at him.

"Will ye tell me what happened?"

"Aye." Masie stood and walked over to him. "I found Leana unconscious with two men in the blacksmith's shop. The men were dead, and Leana remembers nothing."

Kerr exhaled, relived she wasn't the one suspected. Even if she was, it would have made no difference in his decision.

"She does no' remember killing the men?" Kerr asked.

"Nay, and I dinnae believe she did it."

Kerr scratched his chin, pondering the information. "Where are yer sisters?"

"I dinnae know. We were separated when we escaped Raven's Landing."

"Lass, I wish ye would have come to me first." He caressed her cheek.

"I couldn't. I was afraid ye'd send me back to Dornoch."

Silence crept between them. He rubbed his thumb across her bottom lip. No woman had ever made him feel so alive. No woman had ever made him think about the future. There was no way he was going to let her go.

"There's things I want to tell ye about me, but I can no'," Masie whispered.

"Trust in me, Masie." He kissed her forehead. "We all have our demons to slay."

He could see the sorrow in her eyes and the darkness. What had brought such despair upon her?

"What if I'm the demon? Would ye still want to slay me?"

Kerr's dark brows creased. "Ye're no demon. Dinnae be daft." He took her in his arms. "I dinnae want to hear any more of this madness. In the morn, I'm taking ye back to Wickshire where ye belong. Ye are under my protection. Cormag will never get his hands on ye as long as I live."

Kerr claimed her lips with a kiss made to make her insides tingle all the way down to her toes. She was prepared to tell him everything about her true nature, but one smoldering look from his dark gaze and she didn't have the courage. She couldn't risk losing him. Leaving him had left a hole in her heart and she swore she'd never let him go again. Returning to Wickshire with Kerr was all she ever wanted. Mayhap a fairytale, but tonight she'd live in that world, be the woman he thought she was, and experience being loved by a man.

She knew he was a man of his word and would indeed protect her. But she wanted more than protection. This was the man who made her feel alive. Made her feel there was a possibility of true happiness, a clan, husband, protection, and unwavering love.

Masie, ye're not like the mortals. Tell him before it's too late, her pesky conscious warned. Mayhap her fairytale wouldn't have a happily-ever-after, but she would worry about that later. She closed her eyes as he moved his lips seductively down her neck. "Kerr," she moaned.

"Hmm."

"Are ye sure ye want to do this. I think 'tis best we get some rest. We have a long journey in the morn." He grabbed her arse and pressed himself against her womanhood. "Does this feel like I need rest?"

Masie giggled. "Now who's seducing who?"

"Och." In one fluid motion, she was swept off her feet. "Have ye ever been loved properly by a man?" He laid her down on the pallet.

Innocently, Masie looked up into his lust-filled eyes.

Kerr ached a brow. "Nay?"

His hot breath seared her cold flesh as he licked and nipped down her neck. The weight of him on top of her awakened Masie in many ways. The curiosity of seeing him naked, the anticipation of being touched in ways she'd never experienced, her body aching for him—all of her senses were heightened at the same time.

Suddenly, he sat back on his heels, exposing her to the chill. She'd never seen a man naked before, and as he undressed, she couldn't stop staring. Lean, toned muscles rippled down his abdomen. Was she ready for the wicked promise burning in his eyes? Aye, she was ready.

The glow of the candlelight cascading over his skin confirmed indeed he'd been made by the gods. A line of dark hair trailed below his navel and disappeared into his trews. Nervously, she bit her bottom lip and looked up at him wondering if she was truly ready for this.

Kerr smiled as if he was reading her mind. "Dinna worry. I won't hurt ye."

"Never, as long as the stars still twinkle in the sky, would I think ye'd hurt me." His skin twitched under her touch as she followed the trail of dark hair with her fingertips and then began to unlace his trews. She released his manhood. Overtaken by desire, she gripped his hard, long length and caressed him. The skin was so soft.

"Lass, there's nothing more beautiful than watching ye touch me. Yer hands are like magic."

Knowing what she was doing pleased him, only emboldened her. A low growl escaped his lips. Masie stopped. Did she do something wrong? "Did I hurt ye?"

"Nay, but if ye keep touching me like that, I won't have much to offer ye."

He rolled her on top of him so she straddled his body. She lifted the hem of her dress, exposing her thighs. It wasn't enough. She wanted to be naked with him. Fumbling with the ties of her shift, she finally stripped it off.

Masie pulled her long blonde-hair back, giving him a full view of her naked body. He cupped her breasts, squeezing lightly. His thumb caressed her hard nipples, sending gooseflesh up her body.

"Masie Keith, ye're a bonny lass." He sat up and encouraged her to wrap her legs around him, cradling her wanton body against his. He pulled her into a ravenous kiss.

"Tell me what ye want, lass. I'm all yers," he whispered.

She held his lust-filled gaze and trusted her instincts. She guided his hands down her body, taking in every delicious sensation before stopping between her legs. Mayhap a bit bold, but she desperately needed his hands on her.

She hissed as his fingers parted her folds. Masie arched into him, craving more. "Kerr," she moaned.

He growled, a familiar sound she was growing to love. His fingers worked their own magic inside her, falling into a pleasurable rhythm. Every muscle in her body tightened as she raced toward something so pleasurable, she had no words for it. Hot tingles pulsed through her body. Her thighs quivered. Her vision blurred. What was happening to her? She was on the edge of shattering.

"That's it my sweet, wee bird. Let go."

Weightlessness consumed her as she grabbed the furs and held on as a rush of warmth came over her. She felt like a raven flying. Her body was no longer her own. It accepted everything Kerr was giving. "By the saints!" she cried out.

She clamped her mouth shut as she felt the tips of her fangs start to descend. *Goddess, not now!*

She buried her head against his neck, breathing in his scent, which intensified the pleasure. As the sensations subsided, Masie clung to Kerr, her body limp from ecstasy, her mind finally at peace.

Kerr rolled her over and settled between her legs. "Lass, that was beautiful."

"What did ye do to me?"

"I gave ye pleasure."

"Aye."

"And I'm no' done." Kerr smiled. He grabbed her leg and hooked it around his waist. "Are ye ready?"

"For what?"

Kerr arched a brow and positioned himself against her core, pushing ever so lightly.

"There' more?"

"Lass, I haven't even begun." In one fluid motion, he thrusted deep inside, stretching and filling her.

It was the most beautiful thing she'd ever felt. Their connection could never be broken. Kerr belonged to her and she belonged to him. Hugging him close, she marveled at every glorious inch of him. Masie loved him, there was no doubt.

"By the saints, lass," he hissed as her insides contracted around his cock. Slowly, so he wouldn't hurt her, he slid in and out, letting the pleasure build between them. God's teeth, she was tight.

Masie's body tensed and he thought himself a bastard knowing the pain she must feel. "Masie, as much as I want ye, I dinnae want to hurt ye. I can stop."

"Kerr Gunn," she said breathlessly. "Dinnae dare stop."

As if he needed convincing... The desire to please her beyond her wildest dreams drove him to claim her faster. *Shite, she felt so good.*

"'Tis happening again," she moaned.

He grinned like a besotted fool. "Stay wit' me, Masie." He took her lips with a hot searing kiss.

Her body quivered.

"Shite," Kerr hissed. His body jerked as he spilled his

seed deep inside her. Not wanting to lose the intimacy he'd waited so long to establish with Masie, he gently laid on top of her, listening to her heartbeat.

"I've never felt like this before," She said, twirling her fingers in his hair.

Kerr kissed her breast. "Me, either. I can no' get enough of ye. Ye've bewitched me, lass."

"Nay, 'tis ye that has bewitched me. Can I tell ye a secret?"

Propping himself up on his elbows, he stared into her eyes. Her cheeks were flushed—aye, he'd left his mark on her. *Greedy bastard.* "Of course, ye can tell me anything."

"I've dreamed about this. Ye and me sharing something beautiful." She looked away. "'Tis daft. I'm sorry, my head is in the stars."

He cupped her face bringing her eyes back on him. "Lass, ye are no' silly. I've thought of ye many times naked." He balled his fists into her hair. "Underneath me." He kissed her. "Ye hands on my body." He slid kisses down her neck. God's bones, her skin was soft.

"I do need to know one thing?" he asked.

"What?"

"Did I live up to yer expectations?

"Kerr." She smacked his chest playfully.

"I'm serious. 'Tis good for a man's ego to know he pleases his woman in bed."

"Ye've done wicked things to me." She wrapped her legs around his waist. "Show me more."

15

PERCHED on top of his charger, Cormag scanned the valley below. Five hundred of his best men were camped behind him and ready for battle. The cold night air snaked up his spine as he sat watching the cottage nuzzled in the woods. The two hundred Clan Gunn men on the other side of the valley hadn't gone unnoticed.

It pricked his arse that Laird Gunn refused to give up Doughall's daughters. He wanted justice not war, but now they left him with no choice. His heart had grown black with hatred from the loss of his son. Beathen would be avenged. He'd see those girls burn for his son's death and end the curse once and for all.

"My, Laird." Hamish's voice pulled him from his thoughts.

"Aye?"

"When do we attack?"

Nothing would please him more than attacking now, but his gut warned him to tread softly here. He wanted the wench taken alive.

"Dawn. We'll move the first line of infantry as soon as there's a glow in the sky."

"Aye, my laird."

"Inform Commander Rafe to ready his men."

Hamish tuned and began to make his way back to camp.

"Hamish," the laird called out.

"Aye."

"May God favor us and show our enemy mercy, for I will no'."

Kerr awoke with a throbbing erection. He rolled over and ran his finger down Masie's spine. She squirmed and he scooted behind her. By the saints her body was soft as silk. He pulled the hair away from her neck and trailed a line of kisses to her shoulder.

Masie moaned.

He slid his hands under the furs and cupped her breasts, marveling at how perfectly they fit in his hands. Being surrounded in her warmth and his name whispered on her lips had confirmed he'd found the woman he wanted to spend forever with. *Forever?* Aye, indeed, he'd been bewitched.

He pressed his cock against her arse.

"I see someone is awake early." She snuggled against his chest.

"And hungry," Kerr murmured, nuzzling her neck.

"I'm no' much of a cook."

"Miss Sinclair can teach ye. She's a fine cook." He slid his hands between her thighs and Masie shivered.

"Kerr, we need to talk."

"No' now. I want to pleasure ye," he growled as he kissed her.

Masie rolled over, facing him. "I'm serious."

Kerr kissed the tip of her nose. "What bothers ye, love?"

Masie sat up, tucking the fur around her breasts, a worried look spread across her face.

"Lass, is it bad?"

"Do ye smell something burning?"

Dumfounded, he shook his head. "What?"

"I smell something burning." Masie leapt off the bed, taking the fur with her. She darted to the window and gasped.

Kerr joined her.

"Cormag has found me," Masie cried.

Kerr's jaw ticked in anger. A line of Keith men advanced on the cottage. They drew their bows and released dozens of fiery arrows. They landed in front of the cottage, sending out a warning for what was to come.

"Masie, get dressed. We dinnae have much time." Kerr quickly donned his trews and searched the room for his tunic.

Masie slipped on her dress. "Kerr, what are we going to do? We're surrounded."

Kerr grabbed her cloak, wrapped it around her shoulders, and tied it securely in place. "I made an oath to protect ye." He cupped her face. "I have two hundred men close by. They will come to our aid." He kissed her. "Dinnae fash yerself, lass."

Masie nodded.

"We need to leave before it's too late." Kerr sheathed his sword and strode to the door. "Masie, come." He motioned her over. "Keep low and keep moving."

"What if we get separated?"

"We won't. Trust me." He reached down the side of his boot and unsheathed a dirk. "Here." He handed it to Masie. "Dinnae be afraid to use it."

"Aye."

He caressed her cheek. "I love ye, Masie Keith."

Masie smiled. "And I, ye."

Wasting no more time, Kerr cracked the door open. When there was a break in the fiery assault, he took Masie's hand and slipped out the door. Crouching down, they made their way to the side of the cottage, their horses were gone.

A minor setback, Kerr searched the woods where he'd left his men. He prayed they had seen the fire and were on their way, but he had no way of knowing. Kerr must get Masie to safety.

Another round of arrows flew behind them, setting the cottage's thatched roof on fire. The roar of horse hooves pounding the ground surround them. *Shite!* "Masie, run!" He unsheathed his sword and ran behind Masie.

Arrows rained down. Kerr's instincts warned him to look behind them. Two men on horseback charged. They were close to the forest, but Masie was even closer. If he could distract the riders, she'd have a better chance making it to his men.

Kerr halted. Like a true warrior, he raised his claymore and gritted his teeth. "Come on, ye bastards."

Something told Masie she was alone as she ran deeper into the forest. She looked over her shoulder and Kerr was gone. "Nay."

She spun around, refusing to leave Kerr behind. The cottage was engulfed in flames, Keith men on horseback circled the area, searching for her. But where was Kerr? From the corner of her eye, she spied two men on horseback. They were charging Kerr! Horror stricken, Masie watched him slash the legs of a horse, sending the beast to the ground. "Nay!"

Her heart pounded as she ran like the devil toward Kerr. She couldn't leave him alone to defend himself against Cormag's army. It was assured death if she did.

Someone grabbed her from behind and covered her mouth. "Shh. I will not hurt ye."

Masie squirmed, fighting to break free. "Lass, 'tis me," A rough, yet familiar voice whispered. He removed his hand from her mouth. Masie turned around. "Rafe Wulfstan?" Masie said in surprise.

"Aye, lass. I don't have much time. My men are expecting me to bring ye back to Cormag."

Masie shook her head and took a step back. "Ye wouldn't."

"Nay. Adaira would have me skinned alive."

"Have ye seen her?" Masie asked.

"Aye. She's safe."

"What about Leana?"

He shook his head grimly. "We'll find her. But right now, ye need to leave. If I'm caught with ye, I'd be found out. And we all know how Cormag deals with betrayal."

"Aye. But I can no' leave. Kerr is out there and needs help." "Lass, you can't go back. Take my horse and make haste, *now*."

Masie yanked her arm free. "I'll leave, but promise to help Kerr."

"Aye, I'll do what I can."

"Please, I love him."

Rafe clenched his jaw.

She didn't know what had happened between Adaira and Rafe, but one thing was for certain, there had been a lot of heartache. She could see it in his eyes.

"Go. Now," he growled.

Rafe brought his horse to her and placed her on top. "Godspeed." He slapped the charger's arse and the horse took off in a full gallop.

Masie held on for dear life as she weaved between trees, making her way to Kerr's men. She prayed she'd reach them in time for Kerr's sake. Aye, Rafe was a man of his word, but he also had to tread softly. He had connections on both sides of this fight.

Snow fell in thick flurries, making it hard for her horse to make it up the steep incline. Masie tried to steady the horse as its hind legs slipped. "Och, laddie, just a wee bit longer." If her intuition was right, Kerr's men were close.

She reached the top of the cliff and froze. Black and gray tents dotted the forest. Hundreds of men were preparing for battle. Masie pressed on until she reached camp. She dismounted and approached a man saddling his horse. "Where's Bhaltair?" The man tipped his chin to the tent next to them.

Masie raced in. "Bhaltair," she panted.

"Masie?"

"Ye must act fast. Cormag's men are down in the valley. Kerr's there alone."

"Bastards." He strode out of the tent and Masie followed.

"Liam," he called out. "We ride now. Kerr is in trouble."

"Aye." Liam made haste, informing the men of his laird's orders.

Bhaltair stood next to Masie as she watched the gray smoke billowing from the valley. Her heart felt like someone was squeezing it tight. Kerr was a strong warrior, and she knew he was fighting with all his might, but would it be enough? "We must go to Kerr."

"Och, ye aren't going anywhere. Ye're staying here."

Masie glared at him. "I'll do no' such thing. He needs me." She strode over to Bhaltair's horse.

"Nay, lass." He spun her around. "Kerr wouldn't allow it, and neither will I. Ye're safe here. And that's final."

"Bhaltair." Massie looked up at him. "Bring him back to me."

"Aye, lass." He lightly clasped her shoulder, giving her the reassurance she needed. "Dinnae fash yerself." Bhaltair mounted. "My brother is strong."

She watched the band of warriors charge down the cliff. She'd never felt so defenseless before. She should be fighting her way to Kerr.

16

TIME STOOD STILL. Everything around Masie fell into an eerie stillness except for the pounding of her heart. She'd twisted her dress into one big knot as she paced inside the tent. It took all her strength to come in from the freezing snow, for she couldn't tear herself away from the cliffs where she had a clear view of the action below. She didn't want to miss the moment when Kerr returned.

The wind howled and shook the tent, its icy fingers gripping her bones. Masie pulled the fur from a pallet in the corner and wrapped it around her shoulders. Slowly going mad from the long wait, she strode outside. Fresh air would clam her nerves.

The weather had worsened quickly. She braced herself against the wind as she squinted out into a white haze of blowing snow. Kerr had to be coming home to her. Rafe and Bhaltair would see to it. No matter how much she tried to convince herself, the feeling of dread still lingered in the air. After a long while, she retreated to the safety of the tent once more. The hair on the back of her neck bristled just as she entered the shelter. It wasn't because of the cold. Kerr was here, she could feel it.

She hurried outside. A lone figure strode toward her. She felt like her heart was going to leap out of her chest. "Kerr?" Instantly, she took off running. Each step was getting harder and harder as her legs grew tired from treading through the thick snow.

"Masie!"

Wait that wasn't Kerr's voice. She paused, confused. "Bhaltair?"

"Ye shouldn't be out here. Ye'll freeze to death." Bhaltair removed his fur cloak and draped it over her shoulders.

"Where's Kerr?"

Bhaltair shook his head.

Masie looked up at him, unsure what to say.

Rafe strode by holding a body and disappeared inside the shelter.

Tears threatened to fall as she saw the sorrow spread across Bhaltair's face.

"Nay." Masie followed Rafe inside the tent.

At first she wouldn't allow herself to believe the lifeless form was Kerr. He was supposed to be on his feet, welcoming her into his arms. It couldn't be Kerr.

She finally approached the pallet where Rafe had laid the body. She gasped. *Kerr.* Kneeling beside him, she brushed away a strand of dark wet hair stuck to his face. His lips were blue and his skin was pale and cold. As she checked his body for any sign of injury, her whole world threatened to crumble as she spied an arrow embedded in his chest and another in his stomach. She felt for a pulse on his neck. Oh, thank the goddess, he lived.

Kerr turned his head and moaned. "Masie."

She kissed his lips as tears fell down her cheeks. "I'm here, love."

He coughed. "I had to see yer face one last time." He reached up, but didn't have the strength to touch her.

Masie took his hand and kissed it, then placed it on her cheek. "Kerr Gunn, I will no' let ye die," she said between desperate breaths.

He smiled and closed his eyes. "I love ye, my sweet, wee bird."

She had to do something. She couldn't stand here and watch him die. Masie ripped her dress at the hem, forming thin strips of cloth and then laid them next to Kerr. She broke the shafts on both arrows, leaving the heads in place, for she couldn't risk hurting him more.

Bhaltair kneeled beside her and held his brother's hand. "I dinnae care who are what ye are."

Masie gave him a sideways glance. *What did he mean?*

"Lass, ye're no' fooling me. I've felt yer magic."

Masie ignored Bhaltair, acting as if his comment hadn't affected her. She took a strip of cloth and blotted the blood leaking from Kerr's chest.

"All I ask is ye show him mercy like ye showed me." Then Bhaltair stood and left the tent.

Masie met Rafe's steady gaze. "Thank ye for helping me. I know ye took a huge risk."

"Aye, Cormag will be suspicious but it's not him I worry about. Adaira would cut my ballocks off if I allowed anything to harm her little sister."

Masie grinned.

"Lass, this man fought to the death for ye. It's not every day ye find that kind of love and devotion."

A tear rolled down her cheek.

Rafe patted her shoulder. "Cherish his love." He departed, leaving her alone with Kerr.

Not wasting any time, Masie took Kerr's tunic off. She bit her wrist, dripping her blood over the wounds. In a matter of seconds, the barbed arrowheads slowly surfaced from his body. Masie threw the blasted things on the ground, angry someone had tried to take him away from her.

She covered the wounds to help stop the bleeding. She tilted his head back. "Drink, my love."

Her blood streamed slowly into his mouth and he came to life again, color flooding his cheeks as he sucked and licked her wrist like a starving, wee bairn.

Once he had his fill, he fell unconscious. Masie licked her wound, the skin healing instantly. She took the fur from around her shoulders and laid it over his shivering body. Wanting to give him more warmth, Masie slid under the furs next to him. She knew she didn't have much body heat to give, but it would have to do until her blood coursed through his veins. Then his ravaged body would warm from within.

"No one will ever take ye away from me." She snuggled closer, draping his arm around her, holding him tightly. "No' as long as I live." She laid her head on his chest and fell asleep to the sound of his heartbeat.

Through the night the wind howled, shaking the tent violently. Masie had woken intermittently and checked Kerr's bandages. The bleeding had stopped and the wounds were almost healed, yet he was still very cold. She needed to get him back to Raven's Landing where his body would grow strong again.

She tucked the fur around his body. Looking down at him, she brushed his cheek with her fingertips and smiled.

He was going to live. He shivered, and Masie glanced at the fire pit. It had burned down to mere embers.

She flung her legs over the side of the pallet and walked to the fire, placing the last of the peat in the pit. She stood for a moment warming her body and staring into the flames. A vision danced and twisted within it. She was taken back to the night of Samhain.

Out of sight, she'd followed Leana's laughter. Her sister's joy echoed as she pranced and flirted between two men. They made their way into the blacksmith's shop and disappeared inside. Masie ran toward the shop and skidded to a stop just before reaching the door. Gasping in horror, she watched a stream of black mist spiral from the rooftop and disappear into the night sky.

Masie came back to the present and stepped away from the fire. "What the devil was that?" she gasped.

She shook her head, shocked at what she'd seen. What was Leana conjuring? Did she indeed lore those men away to feed or cast some spell? Masie didn't understand everything she'd just seen. It was too real to be a dream.

Kerr moaned and she rushed to the pallet. "I'm here, love."

He opened his eyes and smiled weakly. "Bhaltair was right. Ye are an angel. My beautiful angel."

Masie grinned.

"Come back to bed, I have something to show ye." He winked.

Masie giggled. Her blood had him drunk with lust. "Kerr, ye need to rest."

"Nay, I need to be buried deep inside my future wife."

Masie's eyes grew wide. "Wife?"

"Aye. Will ye do me the honor and become my wife?"

Masie couldn't believe what she was hearing. Kerr

wanted her to be his wife? She wrapped her arms around his neck. "Aye, Kerr, I'll marry ye." She braced her hands on the sides of his face, bent down, and kissed his lips.

He shoved his hands through her hair, pulling her close, deepening the kiss. "I've never needed anyone the way I need ye."

"And I ye. But..."

Kerr rolled his eyes.

"I'll marry ye on one condition." Masie sat back on her heels.

"Lass, I dinnae take well to demands."

She arched a brow.

"What's the stipulation?" he asked.

"If ye feel the same way in two nights, then ask me again."

Kerr eyed her, looking confused.

Masie folded her arms across her chest.

"Masie, I will never understand yer ways, nor do I want to," he jested. "But I'll promise ye this, nothing will change my mind. I'm through trying to make sense of it all. I know what I feel is real and I'm through pushing ye away."

"If 'tis true, then time will make no difference. Ask me again in two nights."

"Aye."

"Brother," Bhaltair exclaimed as he entered the tent and made his way to Kerr's side. "Ye look like shite."

Kerr chuckled. "And what's yer excuse?"

"Och, 'tis good to see ye well."

Kerr looked at Masie. "I have a healer with the most outstanding skills."

Masie blushed.

Bhaltair cleared his throat. "The storm has passed. Are ye well enough to travel?"

"Aye," Kerr grumbled as he fought to sit up. "I'll be ready to ride."

"Easy." Masie helped steady him. "Ye're no' riding anywhere."

"I'm well." Pain creased his face.

"Nay, Brother. Masie is right. Ye're in no condition for riding. I'll have a cart readied for ye."

"I refuse to be hauled around in a cart. I'll make it back home on my own two feet."

This was no time for Kerr to be as stubborn as a mule. Masie shook her head. "What if I ride with ye in the cart?" She wiggled her brows.

Kerr growled and pulled her close. "Hmm, lass." He kissed her. "Ye changed my mind."

"I'll go fetch the cart," Bhaltair said as he quit the tent.

Masie helped Kerr dress, warning him if he didn't stop trying to undress her, they'd never make it back home before the next snowstorm rolled in. Finally, she got him to his feet. Still weak and unsteady, he wrapped his arm around her shoulders. They walked out of the tent to where the cart was waiting. Masie climbed in first, welcomed by a pile of furs. Kerr followed.

Kerr leaned back, resting his back against the wall of the cart. He pulled Masie into his arms. She snuggled up against his warmth. She'd never been so happy in her life. He deserved to know the truth about her. In time, she'd tell him. Mayhap, tomorrow. Maybe in a hundred years.

17

Raven's Landing

Kerr tended to the fire in the hearth, his mind a love-stricken mess. He'd waited two days as Masie had asked and nothing had changed. He craved this lass like the air he breathed. Tonight was the night—he was going to ask her to marry him again.

It had surprised him how easily he allowed Masie to breech the walls around his heart. He considered himself a very lucky man to have her love when he didn't deserve it. He prayed he could be the man she saw in him. A man of honor, her protector, the one who'd spend the rest of his life loving her. Aye, he'd stepped out of the darkness and was ready to give Masie all of himself.

Kerr walked back to the table where Bhaltair was sitting, watching his clan celebrate their recent victory. Word had spread fast about Kerr and his men defeating Clan Keith and how he'd brought his lady home safely.

"Och, Brother," Bhaltair exclaimed and waved him over.

Kerr sat across from him, searching the hall for Masie.

Bhaltair poured a tankard of ale and slid it across the table. "What has ye smiling like a fool?"

Kerr grinned. "I have no idea what ye're talking about." He took a long pull from the mug.

Kerr paused as Masie entered the hall—a vision of grace and beauty. The green and gold dress she wore hugged her frame perfectly, enhancing her full breasts. Her blonde hair was plaited in one long braid that hung down her back, giving him a sensual view of her thin neck. His lips twitched as he imagined kissing and tasting her skin.

Their eyes met from across the room and his blood boiled with desire. Her smile brightened his soul. As she made her way to the table, he watched her hips sway. Aye, she would make a fine wife and mother.

"My laird." Masie greeted Bhaltair with a curtsey.

She sat next to Kerr, giving him a sideways glance as she reached for the pitcher of ale. "Ye look well this eve."

"Aye." He winked as Masie blushed attractively.

Since they'd arrived home, they hadn't left his bedchamber. He couldn't explain the unwavering need to be inside her, but he wasn't complaining.

"Masie," Bhaltair said. "As soon as the storm passes, I'll send a team of men to search for yer sisters. I know ye must be worried about them."

"Thank ye." Masie sipped the ale. "Knowing what Cormag is capable of, I do fear for their safety."

Kerr placed his hand on her thigh and squeezed softly. "I'll personally make sure they make it back here."

Masie placed her hand on top of his and looked up at him. Those blue eyes would always be his undoing. "I have no doubt."

"I only wish I could have gutted the bastard when I had the chance."

"I'm safe here." She smiled.

Aye, she was, and he'd make sure Cormag or anyone else who dared to harm her would pay dearly.

He kept his gaze on her as she sipped more ale. It was time. He couldn't think of one reason not to ask her hand in marriage. Aye, there would be some clan members not happy with his choice, but he knew in time they would accept her. Besides, since when did he give a rat's arse what people thought?

He noticed her squirm and rub her neck, visibly uncomfortable underneath his heavy gaze. "Are ye well, Kerr?"

"Why do ye ask?" He brought her hand to his lips and kissed it.

"Because ye keep looking at me as if I were naked," she whispered.

Kerr smiled wickedly. "That's because I am."

Masie slapped his chest playfully and then sat up straight, acting like a proper lady. "'Tis no' appropriate, Kerr Gunn."

"Och, lass, then let's make it proper. Be my wife."

Masie's eyes widened. *So, this was why Kerr was acting so strange.* Her blood had left his body and she knew Kerr still wanted her to be his wife. She should have seen this coming, but in all honesty, she didn't want her time with him to end. As soon as she told him the truth about who she truly was, he would never accept it. And worse yet, what would he do to her for betraying his trust? Witches were burned alive. What would they do to blood drinkers?

He drew her in like a moth to a flame. "Masie, I'm only going to ask ye once. I can make ye happy."

"Ye do make me verra happy."

"Then marry me."

She nodded. "Aye."

"Aye." Kerr confirmed as if he didn't believe her.

She only nodded, for if she opened her mouth, the truth would fly out and she'd shatter. She wanted to tell him, but the pain she would endure from losing him kept her from being honest. Keeping her secret a wee bit longer seemed better than losing him forever.

Kerr took her into his arms and held her tight. "I love ye, Masie Keith."

"And I, ye." She whispered against his neck.

18

MASIE SPENT the better part of the day in her chamber with her maid and two helpers. They bustled about, pinning and trimming her in extravagant blue silk, for they had no time to waste. Kerr insisted they were to marry by tomorrow eve.

"Mistress." The seamstress took a step back. "Ye make a bonny bride."

"What?" Masie asked as if she had been drawn away from her thoughts. "I'm sorry. It seems my mind is elsewhere."

The woman tsked. "Och, child, no apology necessary."

Masie ran her hands down the dress, admiring the woman's work. She twirled, marveling at how her skin felt against the soft material.

"Careful," the woman warned. "We wouldn't want a pin to prick ye."

Regret crept over her, knowing she was pretending to be someone she wasn't. Her mind spun out of control as she thought about ways to tell Kerr the truth. It was ripping her apart. He deserved to know. She couldn't live a lie no matter how many excuses she desperately wanted to believe. Happiness didn't belong to her kind.

With a heavy heart, she carefully removed the dress and handed it to the chambermaid. "I hope I'll still be the princess who gets to wear this."

The woman gave her a confused look.

Massie donned her regular clothes and left the bedchamber. She had to find Kerr before it was too late. She couldn't marry him without him knowing her everlasting, blood-drinking side. No matter how she presented the truth, she was still a monster.

Masie strode down the corridor in a nervous sweat. Checking Kerr's bedchamber first and knocked on the door. When he didn't respond, she knocked again and opened it. "Kerr?" she called out.

Relived he wasn't there, she closed the door. He must still be out hunting. She'd wait in the great hall for him. From the bottom of the stairs, Masie took in the hall. It was fit for a king. Servants were preparing the tables with sprigs of evergreen and candles. Fresh peat had been placed in the hearth, the roaring fire warming the hall. Vibrant tapestries hung on the walls, depicting stories about Clan Gunn's triumphs, family, and great battles.

"Masie." A woman came her way. *Shite, it had to be her.*

Masie ignored the brunette who had given her so much grief before and walked in the opposite direction. She was in no mood to deal with her. Every time they had an encounter, Masie fought the compulsion to rip the woman to shreds.

The woman blocked her path. Masie stopped, planted her hands on her hips, and huffed in frustration.

"I dinnae want any trouble," the woman stated.

"Then get out of the way." Masie stepped to the side. But the woman blocked her path again.

"Let's start over." She held her hand out to Masie. "I'm Ina."

Masie eyed her up and down, suspicious of her changed behavior.

Ina withdrew her hand. "I wanted to congratulate ye. Kerr is a fine man."

"Aye, he is."

"'Tis a miracle ye were able to heal the laird and his brother. Ye must come from a long line of healers."

Masie raised a brow. "What do ye want? I'm in a hurry."

Ina leaned into Masie. "I'm ill."

Masie's eyes widened. "What do ye mean? Ye look well."

"I've had a terrible fever at night. My head aches all the time."

"Ina, I'm sure it will pass."

"Please, I went to the clan healer. Her herbs can no' help me. I'm begging. Please help me."

Masie studied her pleading face. The lass was being sincere. "Do ye know what ye ask of me?"

Ina nodded and brushed her hair off her neck, exposing a thick vein running from below her ear to her collarbone.

Masie's eyes fixed on her lifeline—her stomach knotted. Depriving herself of blood was dangerous, but she couldn't cross the line. If the lass was ill, her heart wanted to help, but her other side pricked her skin, urging her to drink.

Suddenly, Ina doubled over, holding her head in her hands.

Masie grabbed her shoulders, steadying the lass. "Ina, ye need to sit." Masie helped her to a quiet place next to the hearth. "Here." She helped Ina to a chair.

"Please, Masie, ye must help me."

The pain in her face tore at Masie. "Aye, I will help ye. Can ye make it to your bedchamber?"

Ina rose weakly, then fell back into the chair. "I'm too dizzy.

Quickly, Masie looked around the hall, making sure no one was watching. Thankfully, everyone was too busy preparing for tomorrow's festivities to notice.

Masie scooted a chair in front of Ina and sat looking into Ina's pleading eyes.

"Take the pain away," The woman begged.

Masie nodded. She leaned into Ina's neck, inhaling her skin. Odd, Masie thought, there was no smell of disease or illness. She breathed in deeper and before she could hold it back, the demon inside unleased.

Her gums throbbed as her canines extended. Her fingers wrapped around Ina's neck as she pushed her head to one side, exposing more of Ina's delicate flesh. The urge to drink consumed her, overshadowing the underlying warning.

Ina's heartbeat raced as she pressed her lips against the lass's skin. Masie bit her neck. Ina winced, then settled into Masie's touch. The blood pumping through Ina's veins poured into Masie's mouth. She closed her eyes and sucked harder, allowing the demon to take her fill.

Suddenly, a sweet taste tinged Ina's blood. Ripping herself from Ina's neck, no matter how hard she tried, she couldn't retract her fangs. Masie hissed in pain and clutched her cramping stomach as she fell back into the chair. "Poison? Ye tricked me."

A low laugh escaped Ina's mouth. "Did ye think ye were the only witch in Wickshire?"

Masie slouched lower in her seat. "I dinnae understand."

Ina yanked Masie's head up by her hair until their eyes met. "Before ye, Kerr was mine. I was to wear that dress the seamstress made. I was the one to warm his bed and bear his children. Now he'll see ye for who ye really are."

"Bitch!" Masie hissed. "What did ye do to me?" She struggled against Ina's grip.

"Och, lass." Ina reached into the top of her dress, pulling out a small leather flask. "The potion I mixed was made to keep ye in yer true form. I must confess, I wasn't sure what ye were and if the spell would work. My instincts were right, ye're a bloodsucking Unseelie fairy, a *Baobhan sith*." She threw the flask at Masie.

Dumbfounded, Masie couldn't believe she'd fallen for Ina's trickery. Anger consumed her—there was no holding back the monster. Masie grabbed Ina's hand and twisted her arm until Ina lost her grip on her hair. The wench might be a witch but Masie was more powerful.

"Ye have no right to claim Kerr. He does no' love ye." Masie growled as she pushed Ina up against the wall next to the hearth. "Dinnae ye understand, all magic comes with a price." She wrapped her hand around Ina's throat and squeezed.

"Go ahead, blood drinker, try yer best to kill me. Everyone will soon know the truth and ye'll live yer life rotting in the dungeon—alone."

The beast inside snapped and Masie's powerful jaws clapped down on Ina's neck, crushing her bones. Ina screamed out in harrowing pain.

"Masie!" A stern voice called out from behind her—the voice reached through the violent fog in her mind and went straight to her heart. Desperately, Masie fought to gain control, but the poison was holding her hostage inside her own body.

"Masie, let Ina go."

She lifted her head, listening to Kerr. Blood trickled

down her mouth. She couldn't allow Kerr to see her this way.

"Masie." Kerr approached cautiously. "I'm no' going to hurt ye, but ye must let Ina go."

A low, deep growl escaped her mouth, sending out a warning to stay back. The noise was soul-shaking. She'd never made it before. What if the monster tried to hurt Kerr? In her current state, she was no longer in control and couldn't chance hurting the man she loved.

Slowly, she let go of Ina's neck. The woman dropped to the floor.

"I told ye." Ina looked up at Kerr. "She's a monster."

Masie's heart shattered at the horror she saw on his face. This was not how she planned on telling him but now her secret was out.

Another ripple of pain swam across her stomach. She needed to find a place to hide until the poison wore off. There was no telling what she was capable of doing.

With tears in her eyes, Masie covered her mouth and ran toward the castle doors. She rushed into the bailey and looked back. A small part of her hoped Kerr still cared enough to follow her. That thought dissolved into a painful reality as she watched the double wooden doors close, shutting her out of Kerr's life. Masie swiped a tear from her cheek. She should have told him the truth when she had the chance. Now, after seeing her for who she truly was, he'd never accept her.

19

SOMEWHERE BETWEEN THE evening meal and the rising of the moon, Kerr found himself mindlessly walking the battlements heavy in thought. He'd left Ina with the healer, for there was nothing he could do to help. The healer was hopeful the lass would make it through the night, but prayers were desperately needed. If the loss of blood didn't kill her, infection would.

The wind blew relentlessly as snow flurries collected on his eye lashes, yet he didn't feel a thing. He was in a state of shock. He'd never seen anything quite like it. Masie was evil and yet so delicate.

In a way, he blamed himself for what had happened to Ina. He'd failed in protecting his people. How foolish could one be? He allowed a stranger to capture his heart, and now an innocent woman clung to life. How could he allow this to happen?

The lass he'd fallen in love with was truly a monster. The same woman who'd saved his brother and himself. The lass who had a heart of gold. The kind soul who nurtured

Rabbie like a mother. What could have driven her to unleash such terror? And why, Ina?

Kerr leaned against the stone wall. He looked up at the moon. What was she? An image flashed of sharp white fangs and blood dripping from the corners of her mouth. Her black-as-night eyes looked like they'd seen hell.

Kerr shook her from his thoughts. *Nay, that is not my Masie.*

Pushing off the wall, he trudged to the edge of the battlement and looked down. She was out there somewhere, frightened. He wanted to be sympathetic but he was numb. More than being a monster, she'd lied to him. Mayhap it wasn't the beast at all he loathed, it was the lies. Could he forgive her and accept her dark nature?

Kerr made his way back inside the castle, headed to Masie's bedchamber. He stopped in front of the door and rested his forehead against it. Should he knock or walk away? Was their love worth fighting for? Was Masie worth fighting for? *God's Teeth, be a man and go to her.* He cracked the door. "Masie?" She didn't answer.

He walked over to the hearth, only a glowing ember remained. He placed some peat on the fire. As he looked around, he found Masie's cloak on the bed. He picked it up and smelled it. Her scent wrapped around him. "Masie," he whispered. "Why?"

A wave of anger coursed through him. Furiously, he threw her cloak on the bed, then ran his fingers through his hair. Like his father, he'd been bewitched by a lass, the one thing he vowed never to succumb to. Heartbreak had sent his father to an early grave. Kerr was now in the same predicament. The moment he opened his heart to a lass, she crushed it. What a fool!

Now he was stuck with a decision. If Ina didn't make it

through the night, would he charge Masie with murder or would he turn the other cheek? Should he forgive her and send her away?

Kerr walked over to a darkened corner and sat in a chair. He placed his elbows on his thighs, resting his pounding head in his hands. What was he going to do? He loved her. He sat there for a while, questions he had no answer to plaguing his mind. He leaned back and drifted off to sleep.

Hours later, the creaking bedchamber door startled him awake. A slender form stood in the doorway, her long, blonde hair in tangles. He sat up.

"Kerr?" Masie entered the chamber, twisting her hands together. "Ye must think I am a monster." She looked down at the ground. Seeing the shame written on her face felt like a boulder slamming into him. "I know I haven't been truthful. I didnae know how to tell ye and keep ye."

Kerr glared at her. "Didnae ye think I had the right to know who—" He paused. "What I was falling in love with?"

"Kerr, I'm—"

"Nay." He shook his head and stood. "I dinnae want to hear how sorry ye are. All I ever wanted was the truth."

She walked closer, causing him to take a fearful step back. "I will no' hurt ye. Let me explain."

He kept a watchful eye on her.

"Aye, I'm no' like the other lasses. When I was a wee child, my sisters and I wanted to change our fate. Our father abused my mother terribly and he didnae stop there. He beat Adaira. One night, Leana wished upon a star and the fairy fire appeared. We followed it into the forest believing our fate would change." Masie looked into the flames as she remembered how cruel the queen had been. "We made a deal with the queen. To kill the Doughall, the queen had to gain a life."

"Ye made a deal with a fae? Are ye daft, lass?" Kerr exclaimed.

Masie spun around. "No' daft. Desperate."

The sharpness of her tone sliced through him.

"We stuck together, no' allowing one sister to carry our burden. We had to help our mother. But we didnae know the truth. Our mother kept our true identity from us. The queen lifted the protection spell my mother placed on us that cloaked us from her knowing who we were. We spent ten long winters under the queen's rule. She taught us how to become *Baobhan sith*."

"Then 'tis true, ye are a—"

"Blood drinker. Aye." Vibrant blue eyes met his. "We only feed off the fatally sick and dying."

"But ye healed my brother and I." Kerr's brows creased. "Why didnae ye kill us?"

"Kerr, I would never hurt ye. My blood is not only a curse but a cure. I can heal people who aren't too far gone. Bhaltair was a close call."

"This still doesn't explain yer attack on Ina."

"Och, attack!" Masie exclaimed.

Kerr softened his tone. "I saw ye with my own eyes. Ye bit her."

Masie stood in front of him. This time he didn't flinch. "What ye saw was Ina tricking me. She claimed to be sick and asked for me to heal her. She's no' who she says she is." Masie handed him a leather flask. "She's a witch."

"Masie—"

"Nay, Kerr, ye must believe me. She poisoned me so ye'd see I'm a monster. It was of no coincidence ye happened to walk into the great hall when ye did and saw me attack her. She provoked me. She wants me gone so she can be with ye."

Kerr didn't know what to believe. Fae, blood drinkers, and witches—did they all exist or was he wrapped up in her web of evil lies? He wanted to trust her but refused to go down the same path his father had traveled. *Protect ye heart, fool.* "Did ye have any doing in Laird Cormag's son's murder."

He silently sent up a prayer, for if she had lied about the murder, he wouldn't be able to forgive her.

"Nay. I told ye the truth. We had to flee Dornoch. Cormag had been waiting to condemn my sisters and I. We're an ugly reminder of the past."

"Does he know what ye are?"

"Nay. Only suspicious."

They stood in awkward silence. Kerr wanted to leave but he couldn't make his feet to move.

Masie broke the silence. "There's more."

"Masie." Kerr shook his head. "I dinnae think I can take any more talk about the supernatural."

"I'm sorry, but I've wanted to tell ye everything for so long."

Bloody hell, was he prepared to hear more? What was she going to tell him next? That dragons are real? "Go on."

"The woman in the tapestry."

"Helen?"

"Aye, she's my mother." Masie exhaled nervously. "She's a Seelie fairy."

He shook his head in denial. He'd heard enough. First thing tomorrow morn, he'd have the priest purge the castle of Helen's spirit and any other creature who might be lurking.

"Please." She reached out to touch his face but he grabbed her arm before she could. "I would never hurt ye." He stared deep into her eyes. "I wanted to tell ye, but I've

seen how people judge those who are different. Burn me at
stake if ye must, but I'm no' ashamed of who I am. I hope ye
show mercy and allow me to leave."

He gripped her waist and pulled her close. Resting his
forehead against hers, he brushed her hair away from her
face. "I can no' allow ye to leave." He ran his thumb across
her quivering bottom lip.

After one last sorrowful look at Masie, he strode toward
the door.

"Please, Kerr, dinnae leave this way. We're supposed to
be married tomorrow," Masie pleaded.

With his hand on the latch, he paused and fought the
urge to stay and pretend everything would be all right. It
was all madness and he needed time to make sense of it, if
that was even possible. Before he changed his mind, he
opened the door and walked out.

The chamber door closed as Masie watched Kerr disappear
out of her life. Begging for forgiveness was of no use. He was
gone. She'd never see him again, unless he attended her
execution. Masie hung her head, her shoulders slumped as
she sat on the bed. What was she going to do?

She was tired of running, tired of all the lies. She'd lost
everyone she'd ever loved—her sisters first, and now Kerr.
There was nothing left, so why run?

Masie looked up at the ceiling and exhaled. Tears
trickled from the corners of her eyes, but she didn't give into
the sorrow. A glimmer of hope washed over her, for he never
once said he didn't want to marry her. He hadn't cancelled
the wedding. Could he possibly still love her, *all of her*?

The fire in the hearth crackled and popped, drawing her

attention to the flames. She envisioned herself tied to stakes in the middle of the village square, on display for the angry people who had watched the play. As she looked around the room thinking of the many ways she'd be punished, she glanced over at the wardrobe. The door was slightly open. She leapt off the bed, secretly hoping the door would open into another realm so she could escape this one.

Opening the door wider, she gasped, holding her hand over her mouth. Her wedding dress hung in the wardrobe, beautiful and fit for a queen. She ran her hand down the silky material. The vision of being tied to stakes changed into a happy dream, she was wearing her blue dress and smiling as she stood next to Kerr in front of the priest.

Masie closed the door to that reality. "Nay." She grabbed her cloak. *He still loves me.*

She strode out the chamber, making her way to the north tower. She had to clear her head before she went crazy. Tracking through the thick snow, she barely had enough energy to climb up the stairwell. She finally reached the top. Shielded by stone and rock, the sea winds howled through the lancet windows.

She sat down on a wood bench, leaning against the wall. The cold stone bit into her back. She pulled her legs up and hugged them to her chest as she snuggled deep into her cloak. Aye, it was cold but it didn't bother her, it never had. Before she whisked herself away dreaming about her fairytale wedding and life with Kerr, she had to understand the severity of situation. What was she going to do?

She wasn't going to run. Tomorrow was either going to be the happiest day of her life or the end of everything.

Stars twinkled over the bailey and a sliver of the moon peeked through the darkness. *Darkness.* She embraced it, it was part of her no matter how hard she'd tried to deny it.

The night accepted her for who she was. She took comfort in the shadows, for it hid the truth. Now the truth was out and she had to face the facts that she could very well be going to her grave come the morn. Though the thought of dying should have scared her, it didn't. If she was condemned to death she'd accept her fate, accept the punishment of the flames licking at her skin. She'd accept her kind was evil and evil things deserved to die. She couldn't bear to hurt anyone else.

The last thing she remembered before falling asleep was searching for a fallen star.

A child's laughter awakened Masie. She opened her eyes, trying to remember where she was. She walked over to the closest window. Morn was breaking and another gray day was upon her. Down in the bailey, the inhabitants of the castle were going about their chores. Two wee lasses held hands and danced in a circle. Masie smiled. Aye, there was excitement in the air.

They're probably excited about the wedding.

The realization struck her. Panicked, Masie raced down the stairs, across the bailey, and up to her bedchamber. Not knowing who was waiting for her inside, she opened the door quietly. To her relief, her lady's maid met her with a smile.

"Och, lass, where have ye been?" the woman scolded. "Ye must hurry. Yer bathwater is getting cold." The maid took her cloak.

Masie relaxed a bit, thankful one of Kerr's men hadn't been waiting to bring her to the dungeon.

After her bath, the woman helped Masie into her wedding gown, tying her laces so tight she couldn't breathe. She closed her eyes, calming her nerves, as the maid finished arranging her hair.

"Lass, open yer eyes." The maid handed her a looking glass.

Her hair was braided in long strands and coiled at the top of her head. Her lips were red and her skin was the color of cream with a tinge of pink on her cheeks. Even though she looked beautiful outside, inside, she felt like a monster. She'd lost control and attacked a woman. She hadn't meant to kill Ina, to scare her, aye, but never to take her life. Goddess, she wished her sisters were here. Adaira would know what to do.

The woman placed her hands on Masie's shoulders and squeezed. "They say the devil watches on the other side of the looking glass."

Surprised at the woman's observation, Masie faced her.

"Och, 'tis nonsense." The woman waved her hand, dismissing the tale.

"Mayhap, the mirror reflects the truth, showing who ye are." *A monster.*

The woman stepped in front of her with her hands on her hips, studying her. "Yer a wee nervous, aye?"

Masie looked up.

"Commander Kerr is a good man. He loves ye. The looking glass shows how we look on the outside, no' who we are. Ye control yer own fate and happiness."

Masie smiled. "I hope yer right." She handed the mirror to the woman.

"Nay." She shook her head. "'Tis a wedding gift. Since I do no' have any wee ones of my own to pass it along to, I want ye to have it."

Masie was stunned by the woman's generous gift. Having a looking glass was a privilege. "I'm honored. Thank ye."

"Mary." The woman answered.

Masie smiled at her.

"Now, we must get ye to the great hall. The music has started."

Masie straightened. She was ready to face her fate whatever it be. "Of course." Nervously, Masie stood while the woman draped a fur-lined cloak over her shoulders. Mary's good nature soothed her rattled nerves, enough so she could walk.

As they reached the top of stairs, Masie paused. She couldn't breathe. Nerves were getting the best of her. "Mary, I need fresh air."

"Aye, mistress." Obviously concerned, Mary wrapped her arm around Masie and helped her down the stairs.

They walked by the people gathered in the great hall. Masie couldn't believe all these people were here for her and Kerr. But did they want to attend a wedding or see her burn? Mary caught her as her knees buckled.

"Are ye well?" Mary asked.

Masie straightened. "I'll be fine as long as I get some air."

20

INA WOKE to Kerr standing over her with an icy glare. She swallowed hard and pulled the fur to her chin.

"I want the truth, Ina."

"I-I do no' understand what ye ask of me."

Kerr crossed his arms over his chest. "I'm no' asking. I'm telling ye. Ye will tell me the truth, Witch."

His stern tone made Ina sink into the bed. "Witch?" she laughed nervously. "I'm no' witch."

"Then you'll explain this." Kerr tossed the flask on the bed.

Ina picked it up. She'd been found out. Kerr was too smart for her to skirt around his questions. "Aye." She looked down, fidgeting with the strap on the flask. "I am a witch. I never meant to hurt ye."

"Och, what did ye think was going to happen when you poisoned the woman I love?"

Ina's heart broke a wee bit more with his confessed love for Masie. "Kerr, I wanted to be the woman ye loved." She looked up at him. "Before she came here, ye were mine."

Kerr shook his head. "Nay, lass, my heart was never yours."

"I know now. I saw the way ye looked at her. I wanted ye to look at me that way. And when I found out about the wedding, I was desperate to stop it. I thought with her out of the way, ye'd be mine."

"What were ye going to do? Place a love spell on me?" Kerr growled.

"Nay," Ina said sheepishly. "I know now it was wrong. I am sorry for what it's worth."

Kerr leaned over, inches from Ina's face. "Ye will be punished."

"Please, show mercy. Do no' burn me at the stake." Ina's voice shook fearfully.

"Dear Ina, that fate would be too generous and end for ye."

Two men entered the room and stood at the foot of the bed.

Surprised, Ina clenched the furs. "What's going on?"

"Ina, ye are now charged with murder and treason.," one of the men informed her.

"Wait. Masie is still alive? Kerr, please, ye can no' do this," Ina pleaded as the men pulled her to her feet. Her intent was to show Kerr Masie's true identity, not kill her. She had to be alive. The potion was to last only a couple of hours.

Struggling against the shackles they put on her wrists, Ina was pushed forward. She stopped in front of Kerr. "She's still alive?"

Kerr looked away, not answering.

Ina shook her head. "I dinnae understand."

"Guards, take the witch away," Kerr commanded.

Ina glared long and hard at Kerr, searching for the answer before the guard shoved her out of the chamber.

Once in the dark depths of the dungeon, they forced her into a cell. Her body hit the stone floor. The smell of shite permeated the air. Iron doors slammed shut behind her, making her cringe. Slowly, she rose to her hands and knees.

In the distance, a voice heckled her. "Aye, lass. Crawl over here. I've got something for ye."

Horror stricken, she didn't dare make eye contact. His laughter made bile rise in her throat. How could this be happening?

Ina stood, shuffling to the closest corner. She sat, hugging her knees to her chest. With no shoes on her feet and a thin shift, the cold ran bone-deep. How long was Kerr going to keep her locked down here with the rats? She rested her head on her knees, fighting back exhaustion, but didn't dare fall asleep.

Kerr stood on the edge of the rocky cliff, peering down into the raging sea, reminding him of the rage he felt inside. Dark water sprayed between the rocks. The waves surged, carrying sand and seaweed out to sea, leaving behind a new beginning.

A man with no regrets, he knew the decision he had to make about Masie would change his life forever. Protecting his clan was of utmost importance. He couldn't allow a blood drinker in Wickshire, it wasn't safe. He scrubbed his hand down his face. Try as he may, he couldn't forget Masie.

The snow crunched behind him. The sweet smell of roses alerted him to her presence. He didn't need to turn around to know who was behind him. He felt her. "I know 'tis ye. Do no' walk away."

"I didnae know ye'd be out here. I should leave."

"Nay." He turned to face her and his heart stopped. God's bones, the lass was stunning. The most beautiful bride he'd ever seen. He cleared his throat. "Please, stay."

Masie nodded and stepped closer to the cliff. "The sea is quite beautiful."

"Aye."

"Growing up, I always found meself escaping to the ocean whenever I needed to think. I'd find peace as the waves crashed ashore. 'Tis like all my fears are washing out to sea."

"Aye, as if its washing away all the bad things in our lives."

"Exactly." Masie glanced at him.

"Too bad we'd freeze our arses off if we jumped into the ocean right now," he pointed out.

Masie laughed.

Silence fell over them. No matter how much he tried to forget, Masie was still a monster. He couldn't rid himself from the image of her with blood running out of the corners of her mouth.

But her heart was pure.

"Kerr." Masie faced him. "Is today our wedding or my funeral? I'm willing to accept my fate, for I can no' live without ye."

He watched as a tear rolled down her cheek.

"I know I am unexplainable, an abomination in your eyes."

Kerr's jaw twitched. "Lass, I dinnae know what to think anymore. Ye should have told me sooner and no' lied to me, then I would have been able to protect ye. Ye've put me in a verra difficult situation." He paused. "Masie, my duty is to protect my people."

Masie looked out into the ocean. "I understand."

"And ye, my love, are part of my people. Lass, there will be no' funeral today." He brushed away the tears. "Nothing will change my love for ye. I just needed some time to think."

A smile spread across her lips.

"Wait, did ye think I was going to—"

"Burn me at the stake."

"Masie." His brows creased.

"I didnae know what to think."

"I told ye I couldn't let ye go. Nothing has changed."

"Everything has changed." Masie stepped out of his embrace. "How are we going to make this work when we're completely different. What will yer people do when they find out what I am? Ye know as well as I, Ina will no' stop until she destroys me."

"Ina is no longer a problem."

Masie titled her head, giving him a curious glare. "What did ye do?"

"She confessed to everything and has been charged with treason and placed in the dungeon until I decide what to do with her. Ye're right, she's a witch. And I might have told her ye're dead."

"What?"

"Masie, I was livid with her. I still am. I wasn't thinking straight. Besides, she deserves to squirm a while for what she's done to ye." He stepped in front of Masie, cupping her face. "She tried to take ye away from me. She'll pay."

"Do as ye must. 'Tis no' my place to tell ye how to punish her. But the fact still remains yer people will never accept me."

Kerr looked deeply into Masie's eyes. "Lass, they have already accepted ye. Ye saved the laird of the clan and his brother. I'd say ye're a saint in their eyes. And ye'll be my wife. They will love ye as much as I do."

"I dinnae know," she whispered and looked away.

"Look at me, Masie." He lifted her chin. "What does yer heart tell ye?" Sliding his hand behind her neck, he pulled her closer, claiming her lips passionately. He wanted to stay like this forever, just the two of them. But he knew it wasn't possible. Whatever she decided, he'd agree to it even if it meant losing her forever. He broke the kiss.

"That wasn't fair," she panted. "How am I supposed to walk away?"

"Ye're not." Kerr smirked.

"My heart tells me for the first time in my life I'm truly happy. I feel safe."

He didn't need a priest to marry the woman he loved. Kerr pulled out a blue and green embroidered ribbon. He took her hand in his and began to bind their hands together. "Do ye, Masie Keith, take me as yer husband?"

She looked up at him with her big, blue eyes. "Aye. Will ye have me as yer wife?"

"Aye. I promise to be the man ye deserve for as long as ye live."

Masie chuckled.

"What? I speak the truth."

"I know, love, and yer words are beautiful. Forever is a long time to keep a promise."

"Och, I meant it." He kissed her, sealing their vows.

Instantly, Masie doubled over.

"What's wrong?"

"I-I dinnae know. Ow," she hissed out in pain. "'Tis my stomach."

"Ye need the healer." Kerr picked Masie up and headed to the castle. "Stay with me, lass."

Kerr kicked open the door and strode inside the great hall.

"Kerr!" His brother called out from across the hall. "Ye're late. What happened to Masie?"

"I dinnae have time to explain, she needs the healer."

"Aye. Take Masie up to her chamber, I'll go fetch her."

Kerr nodded and raced up the stairs. This couldn't be happening. He looked down at Masie as she clung to his tunic. "Dinnae go where I can no' follow. I forbid it."

"Kerr," she gasped. "It hurts."

The pain in her face ripped him up inside. "The healer is on her way."

Kerr shouldered the chamber door open and was met by Mary. "Commander Kerr." She nodded. "What ails Mistress Masie?"

"I dinnae know." He laid Masie down on the bed.

"I'll go fetch some water."

Kerr tucked Masie into the furs. Brushing a fallen strand of hair from her face, he kissed her forehead. "I wish there was something I could do."

Masie looked up at him and swallowed. "Hold my hand."

Kerr took her hand and kissed it. There was nothing he could do to take the pain away which left him feeling powerless.

Bhaltair and the healer rushed in.

"'Tis about time," Kerr exclaimed.

"Och, ye try waking an auld sleeping woman," Bhaltair bit back. "She hit me with her broom."

"Serves ye right." She shook her finger at the laird. "Ye didn't knock."

"Can ye two argue about this later. Masie is in dire need," Kerr said.

"Move." The healer pushed Kerr out of her way. "Where does it hurt, dearie?"

"Here." Masie touched her stomach.

The healer pressed her hands across Masie's belly and mumbled words Kerr couldn't understand. He turned to his brother. "What is she saying?"

"I dinnae know." Bhaltair covered his mouth and leaned close to Kerr. "The auld woman is as daft as a drunken fool."

"I heard that." The healer glanced at the brothers. "I'm still spry enough to bend ye two over my knee and beat the disrespect out of ye." She glanced at Masie. "I've known these two eejits since they were wee bairns."

Masie lifted her head. "What ails me?" She clutched her stomach.

"Little bird." Kerr rushed to her. "Ye must lay back. Rest."

The healer leaned over Masie. "Breathe out, lass." She sniffed her breath. "No sign of poison."

"Then wants wrong?" Kerr asked.

The auld woman straightened with a grunt. "I can no' feel anything in her belly." She scratched her wrinkled chin in thought. "No fever. No poison."

"So, what do we do?" Kerr pressed her.

Reaching into her cloak, the healer pulled a black stone from her pocket. "Put this under her pillow. It will absorb the demon afflicting her."

"Masie does no' need any magic," Bhaltair shouted at the woman.

"I'm afraid 'tis all I can do. In the meantime, I'll give the lass something to ease the pain." The woman walked over to a bench in front of the hearth and sat down. Kerr watched her mix some kind of leaves and wine into a bowl. Again, the woman mumbled as she smashed and stirred.

Kerr felt as helpless as a wee bairn. There had to be a way to help Masie, but how? How was he to help her when he didn't know what ailed her? He sat down next to her on the bed and held her hand.

"If I dinnae know any better, I'd think the auld crabbit was a witch," Bhaltair spat.

Witch. That's it, Ina's spell! She was suffering from the potion and there was one person who could cure her, *Ina.* "Masie." He caressed her cheek. "I think I know who can help ye. I'll be right back."

Masie nodded.

"Bhaltair," he called out to his brother. "Stay here with Masie. Do no' leave this room until I return."

"Aye. But where are ye going?"

"I know who's behind this." Kerr leapt from the bed and strode to the door. There was no time to waste. He didn't know how long Masie could keep fighting. Before his brother could ask any more questions, Kerr made his way to the dungeon.

21

SOMEONE WAS APPROACHING Ina with a torch. She huddled close to the wall, hoping if she pressed hard enough the wall would swallow her up. She knew it was only a matter of time until the man sitting across from her made his move. He'd been eyeing her ever since Kerr locked her up. The swine had been licking his lips, undressing her with his one eye.

"Ina," a man called.

"Kerr?"

Chains rattled against the stone floor as she stood. She shuffled into the light. At first she was relieved it was Kerr, but she knew this couldn't be a friendly visit. She had to pay for the wicked deed she'd done.

"Are ye here to kill me?" her voice shook.

"I should be." Kerr stood before her with a grim expression. "Masie is suffering from yer spell."

"Masie?" Ina's brows creased. "Ye told me she was dead."

"She's no' dead. 'Tis beside the point. Yer spell has caused her much pain and now ye are going to fix it." Kerr approached her. "As God as my witness, if she dies, ye'll never see the light of day again."

"Aye. Take me to her. I can help."

Kerr removed her shackles. "Ye better pray Masie is still alive." Grabbing her by the wrist, he escorted her from the dungeon.

Another wave of stabbing pain ripped through Masie's stomach. This time it was more intense, unlike anything she'd ever experienced before. It felt like someone was stabbing her, then setting her insides on fire. Water running down her face pulled her out of the confusing daze. She opened her eyes to Bhaltair squeezing water from a cloth onto her forehead.

"Och lass, ye had another pain. Here, take this." He handed her a bowl of foul-smelling liquid.

"What is it?"

"'Tis for the pain."

Masie drank the mixture, gagging. "'Tis awful."

"I know, but it will ease the pain. At least for a while."

Wiping her mouth with the back of her hand, she looked around the room. "Where's Kerr?"

"He wouldn't tell me, but he said he'll be back with help."

The pain finally dulled and she could rest. Each spell left her weak. Bhaltair pulled the furs over her. "Ye knew all along."

Bhaltair paused. "About what?"

"Who I am or should I say, *what I am*."

"I had suspicions." He winked.

"'Tis no' like ye see one of my kind every day. How did ye know?"

"Remember the day on the battlefield?"

"Aye."

"I remember ye saying to me it was no' my time to go. Ye brought me back from death. I felt the strength of yer blood flowing through me." He took her hand in his. "I dinnae know exactly what ye were, but I knew it was unlike anything human."

"Ye weren't scared?"

"Nay. I knew ye were special, Masie. Ye have the gift of healing. There is no shame in that." He smiled. "Before ye came along, Kerr was headed down a path of destruction. He was an empty vessel and ye breathed life into him. He loves ye verra much."

Masie grinned. "And *I* love him." Masie squeezed his hand. "Thank ye for yer kindness."

"Nay, Masie, thank ye." He kissed her hand. "And welcome to the family."

The chamber door flung open. Karr and Ina entered the room. Masie froze. "What is *she* doing here?"

Kerr strode to her bedside. "She's here to undo the spell."

"The spell? Ye think the pains are from Ina's spell?"

"Aye. It must be. There's nothing else causing it."

"Kerr, I dinnae trust her, nor do I want her touching me," Masie exclaimed.

As Ina approached her, Masie gathered the furs around her and scooted to the far side of the bed.

"Please," Ina said. "I'm sorry for what I've done. Let me help ye."

Masie looked at Kerr and he nodded. "She knows the stakes. She won't hurt ye."

Masie looked at Bhaltair. He nodded. "I trust my brother. If he says Ina won't hurt ye, then she won't."

Regardless of what her husband and Bhaltair thought of Ina, she didn't trust her, but she had no other choice. If Ina caused her aliment, the witch had to break the spell. "Fine." Masie pinned Ina with a dark glare. "If this is some kind of trickery, I'll rip yer heart out."

Kerr stepped between the lassies. "Masie, there will be no need for that. Right, Ina?"

Ina didn't respond.

Kerr spoke louder. "Right, Ina?"

"Aye," Ina agreed. "Masie, lay back and removed the furs. Where are ye feeling the pain?"

Masie did as she was asked, then rubbed her hand across her stomach. "Here."

Ina stood over her, placing her hands an inch from her stomach. Masie watched as she closed her eyes and whispered in a language she didn't know. *Damn witches.*

Ina moved her hands back and forth Was the spell reversible? There was too many question fluttering around in her head. She couldn't keep quiet any longer. "Ina, what do ye see?"

"Shh." Ina whispered.

Masie exhaled and looked up at the ceiling.

Ina's eyes flew open.

"What?" Masie asked with concern. "Tell me."

Ina stepped back from the bed, clearly shaken.

"Ina, please, tell me," Masie pleaded.

Ina wrung her hands together. "'Tis fairy magic. Dark Unseelie magic."

Masie gripped her stomach. "What do ye mean?'

"My spell is gone. The fae are calling ye home."

"It can no' be." But it was, the pain she felt was the same

pain she'd experienced ten winters ago when the queen stopped her from running to her mother. She'd never forgotten it. Dread filled her heart. She'd thought she'd escaped the queen for good. As long as she resided in the human world, she and her sisters were supposed to be safe from the queen.

"Is there a way to block it?" Kerr asked.

"There is. But—"

"What?" Kerr interrupted.

"I know a spell that can cloud the magic, but not entirely. Fae magic is strong, especially from an Unseelie."

"Then ye must go now and do whatever witches do to conjure a spell." Masie heard the dubious tone in his voice.

Kerr was trying to understand it all. Witches, fae, and now he was married to a blood drinker. Aye it could drive a rational man to madness.

"I'll go with Ina and make sure there's no trickery." Bhaltair glared at Ina.

"Thank ye, brother."

Bhaltair and Ina left the bedchamber.

Masie felt Kerr's gaze on her. She felt guilty for bringing such darkness upon him and his clan. Queen Galanthus Snowdrop was as twisted as a blackthorn's roots, destroying everything for her own gain. Powerful beyond measure, the dark court was a force one didn't disrupt.

A memory flashed.

She was back in the fae world and it was her sixteenth birthday. Queen Snowdrop invited the whole realm to celebrate. At least that was what she believed. Nothing, not even her sisters could have prepared or protected her from what had been planned.

The eve started perfectly when she entered the great hall in her black shimmering gown. The hall was filled with faes dressed for a ball. A group of five men played soft, beautiful music as the crowd formed two lines, separating the men from women.

A man with black hair tied in a tail at the nape of his neck, stepped in front of her and bowed, offering her a dance. Masie remembered how flattered and nervous she had been as he took her hand and lead her to the middle of the room. He presented her to the queen's royal court like a prized possession. Masie searched the throng for Adaira and Leana.

As they reached the end of the dance, they separated into two rows facing each other. A new song began. This time, the tempo quickened and the dance began.

The music stopped and everyone bowed to her as they backed into the shadows, leaving her standing alone in the middle of the hall. She franticly whipped around, wondering what had just happened.

The sound of applause forced her to focus on the front of the hall. The queen sat in a blackthorn throne on a dais, dressed in black, clapping her hands. Flanked by three fae princes who were tall and regal. Behind the queen stood Adaira and Leana, staring at Masie.

The queen motioned to her guards. Before Masie knew what was happening, the five bards were thrown on their knees before her. The queen walked over.

"My dear sweet, Masie... Isn't she the most beautiful thing you've ever seen?" she asked the crowd.

Her subjects agreed.

"Mother, I dinnae understand. Why are these men on their knees in front of me?" Masie whispered.

The queen cupped Masie's face causing her to shiver. "It's time you become one of us. You want to be just like Adaira and Leana, don't you?"

"Masie, nay!" she heard her sister cry out from the dais. "Ye dinnae have to do it."

She looked to her sisters. One of the fae princes dragged Adaira away.

"What are ye going to do with her?"

"Never mind her. Today is yer day. Today yer human side is laid to rest and ye become the Baobhan sith" The queen walked over to one of the musicians and yanked him up by the hair. The man soiled himself, urine dripped down his leg and formed a puddle on the floor.

"Please, dinnae hurt him," Masie begged. "He's done nothing wrong."

"Oh, my sweet." The queen chuckled. "This human isn't here to be punished—he's your feast."

Masie hated her, but couldn't look away.

"You have reached the age where you'll finish the final stage of becoming a blood drinker. Once you feed, your human side will die." She raised her hand, five silver, sharp-as-a-dagger nails shined in the candlelight. With one swoop, the queen slashed the man's neck. Blood poured from his body. "It's in your blood, Masie. Drink."

Masie shook her head. Was this what her sisters were protecting her from? The irony smell of blood heightened her senses, sending a shooting pain up her jaw as her fangs descended. She held her hand over her mouth, fighting the urge to bite the man.

"Don't fight it. It will only make the pain worse," the queen warned and released the man on the floor.

Masie ran over to him and dropped to her knees. She looked into his eyes as he clung to life. "Please, show mercy," he begged.

It broke her heart to see him suffer. There was nothing she could do but end his anguish. Masie lifted his head up from the floor. "I'm so sorry," she whispered as she gave into the beast and clamped her mouth around his slashed skin.

At first, the thought repulsed her. But as soon as the crimson *flowed into her mouth, it awakened something wicked inside her. She sucked on his neck viscously, until she felt his heart stop beating.*

When she was done, she tossed the body aside and set her sights on the next man. She stalked the poor trembling fool with her eyes, then as quick as lightening, pounced on him, sinking her teeth into his flesh.

"Good girl," the queen approved as she took her place back on her throne.

"Masie." Kerr's voice snapped her out of her nightmare.

She shook her head. "Aye."

"Where have ye been? I've been calling yer name."

"You dinnae want to know."

Kerr sat on the edge of the bed. "Ye have to tell me what I'm up against so I can defend ye."

"Nay," Masie exclaimed, shaking her head. "The queen is too powerful. I'll go and face the queen."

"Nay," Kerr roared. "Ye'll do no such thing."

"Ye dinnae understand, I have to go." Masie swung her legs across the bed and stood. Her knees buckled and Kerr caught her before she hit the ground. She wrapped her arms his neck, sobbing. "What if she has Adaira and Leana?"

Kerr held her tight, caressing the back of her head. "Shh. Dinnae fash yerself. We will find them. I have my men out right now looking." He pulled back and took her face in his hands. "Ye do trust me?"

"Aye. With all my heart," she whispered.

"Then let me handle this. Dinnae make me lock ye in yer bedchamber, because I'll do it if it means ye'll be safe."

Masie chuckled.

"We're husband and wife now. We need to start our life together."

"Ye can no' ignore the queen. She always gets what she wants."

"No' this time." He kissed her. "Ye're mine. I'd battle the devil himself if it meant ye'd be safe."

"I love ye, Kerr Gunn."

"And I, ye." Kerr kissed her again. "Now, scoot over. We're getting some rest until Ina returns with the spell."

Kerr slid under the furs, tucking Masie close to his side. He wrapped his arms around her, kissing the top of her head. "I'm never letting ye go, lass."

Masie relaxed in his arms. She felt like they could conquer the world, even an evil fae queen.

BOOK 2 DEADLY DARKNESS - SNEAK PEEK

CHAPTER I

Today was the day her life would end, Adaira felt it bone-deep as she ran through the glen like the devil was coming for her. For a fortnight, the dark fae prince had chased her in the woods, hunting her like prized game. He'd worn her down mentally and physically beyond exhaustion. She didn't know how much longer it would take before he stripped her of the will to live—to fight for what she believed in.

The prince played cat and mouse to perfection—leaving no doubt who the mouse was. One minute she'd be within his icy grip thinking she'd be returned to the queen, and the next, the prince would let her go—prolonging the inevitable for his own twisted amusement.

Hope of making it out of the glen alive was fading, but Adaira held on to the one thing that made her fight—her beloved sisters. They were depending on her.

The thought of her family gave her strength. She stopped and looked behind her. Although she was no longer being chased, it didn't mean she wasn't being followed. She dashed behind a tree, hoping to outwit the devil.

She leaned her head back and prayed the prince hadn't seen her. Her heart thundered as she anticipated another attack. Just the thought of returning to the Unseelie queen tattered her willpower. It was as if the queen was clawing at her, dragging her back inside a nightmare. A nightmare that Adaira had lived through for the past ten years.

Suddenly, something wet slid down her leg. Lifting her dress, she rubbed her calf. Blood soaked through her wool stockings and onto her hand. *Maiden, Mother, Crone?* She searched her body to find where the blood was coming from. A sting spread across her back and she reached over her shoulder, wincing as she swiped at her skin. Shite, the bastard had gotten her. It wouldn't be long until the fae poison entered her bloodstream where the bastard had slashed her back with his claws. She was doomed.

Adaira hung her head. That's when she noticed the bloodstained snow. The trail of blood led straight to her location. Nay! What was she going to do? The prince would surely find her now.

The earth suddenly shifted, causing her to freeze. No mere mortal would have felt it. The air around her flickered like a flame. The hair on the back of her neck stood on end from the powerful charge. He's here. There was no time to react; the prince swooped down from the sky and landed a few yards from the tree. Terror streaked down her spine.

He settled his great black wings and searched the area with his keen gaze. Adaira sucked in a breath, standing as still as the dead. The prince scooped up a handful of blood-soaked snow and inhaled deeply. Her essence was everywhere—the bastard would find her.

Adaira hugged the tree tighter, murmuring the only words of protection she could think of, Maiden, Mother, Crone. Spare me. Or just let me die before he finds me...

She gasped for air, finding the courage to fight. Surrendering wasn't an option. She needed to think clearly on how she was going to escape. Weak from blood loss, her muscles ached. Though she possessed unnatural strength, she wasn't immune to pain and suffering. And the wet cold had finally taken its toll. She needed rest and warmth—shelter from the prince.

The sound of snow crunching beneath his boots echoed around her. He was so close she could hear his heartbeat.

Oh, goddess, please. Please do no' let him see me. She closed her eyes and pressed herself flatter against the tree. The rough bark bit into her flesh like jagged teeth.

The prince crept past her like a fine mist floating through the glen. She cursed herself for being weak. If she had half her strength, she could attack him, rip his throat out, and personally deliver it to the queen. That wasn't going to happen. Instead, she had to outsmart the fae. She'd die before she'd allow him to bring her back to the queen.

Taking in a shallow breath, she eyed him again. He'd moved several feet ahead, studying the trees and ground in front of him. He knelt and scooped up another handful of snow. Adaira welcomed the distance between them, though it wasn't far enough.

Mayhap she'd live to see another night.

He stood and looked up into the sky. Slowly, he tilted his head from side to side like he was listening to something or mayhap someone. Fearing for her life, Adaira slowed her breathing as she kept her eyes pinned on the prince. He spread his massive black wings, stretching them wide. *What is he doing?* He knew she was here and weak. Why hadn't he gone in for the kill?

He crouched down, and with one pump of his wings, he flew up into the sky disappearing behind the clouds.

Dearest Maiden ... she sighed in relief as she peeled herself from the tree. She coughed through the coldness in her throat. On shaky, weak legs she took a step forward, then collapsed into the snow. Her body was shutting down. All she wanted was rest; however, if she surrendered to exhaustion she'd surely die. The prince didn't give up on his prey this easily. He'd return—she had to keep moving.

With all her might, she found the strength to stand. She brushed the snow off her dress and straightened her spine. "Leana, I will find ye."

The day turned colder and darker as the graying clouds engulfed the sky. She shook her head as she continued trudging through the snow. The fae poison was slowly dulling her wits. It would kill her if she didn't tend to her wounds quickly. She couldn't remember how many days she'd been on the run, but the growing pain drove her to find shelter.

Adaira stopped abruptly and squinted through the snow flurries. Smoke billowed up ahead. *Where there's smoke there must be fire, and where there's fire, there must be shelter.* Could she trust what she was seeing? Or was this fae poison trickery? At this point, she hadn't any choice. If she didn't get the poison out of her body, she'd die. And if she stayed outside in the cold much longer, she'd perish from exposure.

Adaira forced her exhausted body to keep going. Black and silver tents dotted the landscape. She heard men's voices in the distance. Aye, this was a campsite, but whose? Why were they camped in the middle of nowhere?

She crept to the closest tent, the fire more inviting than anything she'd ever seen. Keeping watch, she warmed her hands over the flames. Her body slowly tingled back to life as she prayed this wasn't a dream, that she wasn't lying in the snow somewhere dying.

But death visions didn't include the smell of smoke or fine ash drifting high in the nighttime air. This had to be real.

The frigid wind shook the tent, startling Adaira. She quickly retreated into the shadows, waiting to see if anyone would come out. She shivered, imagining herself inside the shelter, tucked beneath a thick fur with a bowl of hot broth in her hands. Her knees buckled. The poison smoldering in her veins was spreading. Someone had to be around to help her. Were these honorable men or beasts like the prince? Would they assist her?

Before she collapsed from exhaustion, Adaira staggered through the snow to the tent and walked in. "Hello?" The word came out as a mere whisper.

When no one answered, Adaira stepped deeper inside. She rubbed the cold from her arms as she looked around. A fur pallet was situated on one side and a sword and water skin were laid out next to it.

Another sharp wind rattled the canvas, but this time it was different. It howled with warning. Adaira's gaze zigzagged across the shelter as the shadow of a wolf appeared on the outside. Consumed with fear, she knew she didn't possess the strength to fight. She moved quickly, grabbing up the sword, ready to strike if she had to. But the beast was nowhere to be seen.

This wasn't over. It couldn't be. Wolves were as relentless

as the dark prince. The bloody bastards hunted in packs and didn't give up—not until the hunt was over—until their prey was dead. Adaira wasn't ready to enter the barren realm of death— she'd fight. If they wanted her, they'd have to come and get her.

A wolf howled and three more shadows appeared, circling the tent. "Show yerself, wolf," she cried out with the last bit of strength she possessed, the sword almost too heavy to lift.

She followed the shadows around the inside of the tent, ready to pierce their furry flesh through the heavy material. Her back was facing the tent's entrance when a cold blast of air rushed inside. A wolf had entered the tent. She felt its breath on the back of her neck.

Heeding her instincts, Adaira whirled around, the sword raised high in the air. A gray wolf stalked closer, snarling and snapping at her. *Shite, the poison.* Would she even be able to swing the heavy weapon? Surely the beast could sense her weakened state and smell her fear. Any sudden movement would invoke an attack.

Too weak to hold on to the sword, it dropped from her hand. The beast lunged and she squeezed her eyes shut, ready to feel its sharp teeth bite into her skin. When she didn't end up on the ground with the wolf gnawing at her neck, she opened her eyes and gasped.

The world was spinning as she staggered forward, finding a naked man with long dark hair streaked with gray standing in front of her. She reached out and touched his face, burying her shaking fingers in his thick beard. Familiar silver eyes bore straight through her. By the saints, she knew those eyes, for they haunted her dreams.

"Rafe?" She swayed and fell forward. Strong arms caught her, pulling her into a wall of pure muscle and warmth.

"My heart's queen." The rugged voice she knew so well soothed her aching body. His words assured her safety. "I will take care of ye."

Adaira rested her head on his chest, letting him hold her up. "Rafe," she swallowed, struggling to talk. "Poison."

"Shhh, let me take care of everything."

Adaira's world faded into a black void, but her heart was safe.

About Victoria Zak

Victoria Zak is an internationally bestselling author in paranormal romance, Scottish historical romance and contemporary romance. Her first book, Highland Burn was runner-up for the InD'tale 2015 RONE award for best paranormal romance.

Victoria lives in the sunshine state with her husband, two beautiful children, and two furry friends. Living in paradise, being a stay at home mom, and to be able to share her stories has been a blessing.

Victoria loves to hear from her readers. You can connect with her through the links below:

www.victoriazakromance.com
victoria@victoriazakromance.com

MORE BOOKS BY VICTORIA ZAK

Guardians of Scotland Series:

Highland Burn

Highland Storm

Highland Fate

Highland Destiny

Daughters of Highland Darkness Series:

Beautiful Darkness

Deadly Darkness (2018)

Wicked Darkness (2018)

Hell's Cowboys Series:

My Immortal Cowboy

Stand Alones:

De Wolfe's Honor

Once Upon a Winter Solstice

The Jewel of Grim Fortress

Midnight's Kiss

www.ingramcontent.com/pod-product-compliance
Lightning Source LLC
Chambersburg PA
CBHW032143170626
46808CB00006B/2351